Other books by Susanne Gervay

I Am Jack
Superjack
Always Jack

Butterflies

BEING

Susanne Gervay

Jack

Illustrated by Cathy Wilcox

Kane Miller

A DIVISION OF EDC PUBLISHING

First American Edition 2015
Kane Miller, A Division of EDC Publishing

First published in English in Sydney, Australia by HarperCollins Publishers
Australia Pty Limited in 2014. This North American Edition is published by
arrangement with HarperCollins Publishers Australia Pty Limited.

For information contact:
Kane Miller, A Division of EDC Publishing
P.O. Box 470663
Tulsa, OK 74147-0663
www.kanemiller.com
www.edcpub.com
www.usbornebooksandmore.com

Library of Congress Control Number: 2014949835

Manufactured by Regent Publishing Services, Hong Kong
Printed May 2015 in ShenZhen, Guangdong, China

1 2 3 4 5 6 7 8 9 10

ISBN: 978-1-61067-455-3

To my lifelong friends
author Moya Simons and artist Jules Sevelson,
who have shared the journey of *I Am Jack*.

Chapter 1

Lights On!

I twist the lightbulb into its socket. Mum yelps. I look down at the bottom of the ladder. She's so excited that I'm changing the bulbs that she's doing a lopsided jumping jack. Mum just can't get the hang of them. The last time she tried to change one, the house nearly blew up. The fuse exploded, lights went off, Mum was zapped. She's now banned from touching anything electrical.

"What would I do without you, darling?"

"We'd live in the dark, Mum." I laugh. "And don't call me darling."

"Oh, I forgot, darling."

I give up. Mum whirls around, nearly knocking Nanna over. I just make it down the ladder in time to catch her. Her teeth slip out, but she's fast and sucks them back in. She beams a Nanna beam. "I can always count on you, Jack."

My sister, Samantha, bounces in with her new puppy and dog Ollie woofing behind them. The puppy has a squished face. It's a boxer cross. I don't know what it's crossed with. Maybe a cow? Ha-ha. Of course Samantha bumps the ladder just as I'm trying to pack it away.

"Watch out." I nudge her out of the way, while her puppy, called Puppy — what an original name — lunges for my shoelaces. I nearly trip over and land on Rob, who's just arrived with a gigantic thermometer.

By the way, Rob is officially my stepdad. He thinks he's very cool. Not sure about that.

"We'll all know the temperature now. Hot or not. Ha!" He checks his thermometer.

I give him a you've-got-to-be-joking stare.

Mum's panting and stares at Rob's head. "Have you had another haircut, Rob?"

Haircut? Rob looks like a tall, prickly bowling ball in a Hawaiian shirt. I'm growing my hair. I don't want to look like a prickly bowling ball. I shaved off my hair to support Mum when she was sick. A shudder runs through me and my stomach knots. Hey, she's not sick anymore and I *need* hair.

Rob rubs his head, smiling. "Good value. I won't have to have another haircut for months."

Mum scrunches her face, unimpressed, but before she can comment, Samantha races towards Rob, just missing Puss, who leaps onto the side table, knocking over Grandad's photo.

Nanna waddles as fast as she can to save it and knocks over Mum and Rob's family wedding photo. I grab it. We're all in that photo, looking like sun-crazed penguins in black suits with bright-yellow shirts and spotted ties. Well, the girls don't look like penguins. More like angels, except Samantha who's too annoying to be an angel. Anna's my best friend and almost part of the family. She's never annoying. In the photo Nanna beams, holding her open locket showing the picture of Grandad. There couldn't be a wedding without him. I put down the wedding photo.

"Lights are working now, Mum. Got stuff to do. Got to go." I head down the hallway, look back to see Nanna rearranging the photo table. Mum's waving a mop. Samantha's squealing, "No, Puppy, no!" Puppy's not listening and is weeing on the kitchen floor. I try not to laugh out loud. I promised Samantha I'd make a bigger doggy flap in the back door so both Ollie and Puppy can get through easily. I've got to do it soon.

I shut my bedroom door. Hector, my white rat, gives me the I'm-starving glare. I crumble a few cookie crumbs. Since Nanna's favorite food of all time is cookies, there's always a supply of them. I have my own personal cookie jar, thanks to her. I grab a chocolate chip one for myself.

I head for my windowsill. Ponto's looking good sprouting there in his jar. My experiment of grafting an onion onto an old potato is a monster. Green shoots spurt from the top. Maybe Ponto can feed the world one day? I've just got to clone him. I've had a lot of failures — and rotting potatoes stink. Worse than stink. I laugh. "But a scientist has to go *where no man has gone before. Captain James T. Kirk, captain of starship USS Enterprise.*" I grab my camera and take a few shots of the alien Ponto for my photo wall.

My wall is looking great. I've enlarged one photo of Nanna showing off her purple glow-in-the-dark underpants. She loves those underpants and bought some for *all* of us. Unbelievable. Has Nanna no idea? I don't wear them, that's for sure. They were super cheap — Nanna said she got them nearly for free. There's a reason for that. I think free is paying too much.

There's my favorite photo of Mum and me. We're both bald as lizards. She hated losing her hair with the chemo, but when I shaved mine off, she cried. She said that I shouldn't have done it. But I could see it made her feel better because I did that for her. As if I wouldn't. Mum's hair's grown back now into a fluffy blond fuzz. Next is the photo of Anna in front of the Napolis' Super Delicioso Fruitology Market. She's laughing, holding a yellow mango, dripping juice between her fingers. She looks so beautiful. My aim was just right: when I clicked, the sun was coming through her long black curls.

I put my camera back on the shelf next to Grandad's old camera. I've used it a few times, even developed old photos. He had a heart attack just before my eighth birthday. I'm nearly thirteen now. I miss him. I glance at the photos of him and me camping. Hey, Grandad, check this out. I look through my telescope and out the window into the sky. Going to be a quarter moon tonight, Grandad.

OK, got to get back to work. My out-of-bounds table — that means *no* Mum, *no* Samantha, *no* Nanna, *no* Rob and *no one* touches it. I've got a soundboard organized, electronic parts, and soldering equipment. Just need to get the speakers working. Need a bit more room. Might have to finish it on my workbench in the shed.

"Jack. Jack." Samantha bangs on my door. She sticks her head through. "Dinner."

I look up. Can't believe it's already dark, though now that I think about it I'm starving. "What's cooking, Sammy?" No answer as she runs off with Puppy trailing behind her.

Nanna's wobbling from her bedroom to the table. She loves food and gives me a toothy smile. She still has her teeth in, which is good. She calls out to me. "Spaghetti Bolognese for a growing boy."

"That's me. Growing."

Chapter 2

Clean Socks

I jump up just before my alarm rings. 5:27 a.m. *Buzzzzz* — 5:30 a.m. I've programmed my brain to beat the clock. Winner — Jack. Loser — Clock.

Jeans, T-shirt, socks. Where are my clean socks? I look under my bunk. Dirty socks. I slide under the bed and grab them. Four pairs. They smell. I aim for the laundry basket and get them in. Bull's-eye. Four pairs of socks, right into the basket. Anna's going to be so impressed when she sees me kick those winning goals. Socks, socks, socks. Ah! Find a clean pair at the back of my drawer. I race out of my room, through the living room, wave at Mum, who's up early as usual.

"I'll have breakfast ready when you're back."

Mum's voice follows me as I leap two steps at a time down the back porch, jump onto my bike, clip on my helmet and zoom out for my paper route. The light flickers through the trees as I cut through the park. I'm flying as I jump dirt potholes, swerve around corners, pedal as fast as I can towards the beach cliffs. Panting, I just catch the sun rising over the sea. Sometimes the ocean's wild, with the winds nearly blowing me down. Sometimes it's flat like glass. Today, there's a juicy swell that rolls onto the sand. There're a few surfers out there already.

I watch until the sun is up, then jump back onto my bike and race down the cliff track to the strip mall. I collect my newspaper stack and get going on my route, throwing them into front yards, on porches and unluckily sometimes onto roofs.

"Home!" I shout as I dump my bike against the shed. Rob's hung up his punching bag just under the metal awning. I give it a whack and race into the house.

"Breakfast." Mum's blond hair frizzes as she swirls around with a plate of bacon and eggs.

Rob's already eating his. "How about me dropping you and Sammy at school this morning? Sammy's dog project looks pretty big."

Mum's eyes go all dopey. "That's so lovely of you, Rob."

Rob straightens up, gives a serious nod of his head to Mum, trying to look like a real dad. I try not to laugh. Rob's real son, Leo, lives up north with his mum. He doesn't come down much, but Rob calls him a lot. Leo's OK. He's nearly thirteen like Anna and me. He calls Rob "Dad." Always feels odd when I hear that. "Hey, Dad," I say under my breath. Dad. Rob. Dad. Rob. Rob. Dad … No, you're Rob. I have this tiny photo of my real dad with Mum and Samantha and me. The photo's in the bottom corner of my photo wall. A pain shoots through my head. I remember:

… The day my dad left, I was five. He had brown hair like me. He wore jeans and a gray jacket. Mum wore

a bright flowery dress and was crying. Samantha was holding on to Mum. I stood next to Mum. Dad shouted: "Said I'm not coming back."

Then he looked down at me. "You be good, Jack."

He turned and strode away. I reached out my hand for him, but he was gone. Then I felt Mum's hand take mine.

Sometimes I think he's walking down the street. I race up behind him, except it's never Dad. But he told me to be good, like he's coming back. Maybe he couldn't come back. Got sick or something. Maybe he'll just arrive at the front door. To see Sammy and me. One day I told Mum that I thought I saw Dad, and she cried, so I've never mentioned him again. Dad doesn't even know that Mum was sick and that we could have been alone. Anyway, I don't care. We're fine without him.

Samantha squeaks and I look around. She's tickling Rob's prickly head at the table. Rob gives Mum a wink. "Nice haircut, hey?" Mum shakes her head.

Rob gets up and strides to the sink to do the breakfast dishes. That's his job. Mum cooks. Rob washes. He thinks he's the only person who can scrape and clean and make those plates sparkle. Have to admit that he always finds the dirty spot everyone misses. He's king of the dishes. I take my dirty plate and glass over to the sink.

"Do you want a hand, Rob? Drying." I grab a dish towel.

He nods and says with a serious voice, "Sure, Jack." He really is trying to be a dad role model. I don't need a dad. But yeah. He's not a bad sort of stepdad.

"Dishes done," Rob announces. "See you tonight, babe." He kisses Mum and calls out, "Let's go," as he dashes to his van.

I shout, "Come on, Sammy."

She arrives in the kitchen carrying her dog project with Puppy tugging at her shoes. Ollie's trying to stop Puppy. Samantha's the shortest eleven year old in her class. Mum says she'll have a growth spurt later like Mum did. Well, Samantha hasn't had one yet and her project is a huge papier-mâché model of a dog that looks like an elephant.

"Hey, that's a good elephant."

"It's a dog," Samantha squeals, stumbling over the size of it.

"That's what I said. An elephant."

Laughing, I grab her project and carry it to Rob's surfing van. Coolest van ever. It's bright yellow with a blue wave splashing down its side and a black velvet interior. Curly writing over the wave says, *If it swells, ride it.*

Rob gave Mum his nearly new super-fantastic four-wheel drive. He said he wanted Mum to have a reliable car, especially after she got sick, because she sometimes comes home late from work at the library. But Rob had a plan all along. He drove the bright-yellow secondhand surfing van down our driveway a day or two after he gave Mum the keys to his other one. "Needed wheels myself," he told her. (Her mouth was open so wide she looked like she was catching flies.) Best van ever.

Samantha plonks herself in the front seat of course. I sit in the backseat, next to her dog-elephant. I look around the van with its black vinyl panels. They are pretty great. Two miniature surfboards dangle from the rearview mirror. There's a new square black-and-white sign on one panel:

GET IN. SIT DOWN.

HOLD ON. SHUT UP.

"New sign, Rob?"

"Follow those rules and life's pretty easy, Jack."

"Hold on. SHUT UP." I grin.

Rob looks in the mirror and chuckles. He turns on his surfing music and revs the engine. A few farts blurt from the exhaust and we're off. Mum and Nanna wave good-bye as "Surfing USA" blares out of the windows.

We drive along the ocean cliff road. I check out the surf. Rob swerves left, past bushland. A couple of dogs run out of it, snapping at the van's wheels. Then there it is, Boat Harbour School.

Rob waits with the engine idling as I drag Samantha's dog-elephant out of the backseat. Samantha runs around to check what's happening and I pretend to drop it. She squeaks and her ponytail bobs. She looks pretty funny. "So where do you want it to go?"

"The library. Come on, Jack."

George Hamel gives us a smirk, but he leaves me alone these days. He wouldn't bully me now. I wouldn't let him.

Comments and howls fly across the school yard from that idiot Winger Ratko and his mates.

"How's Jumbo?"

"Carrying a load, Jack?"

"Ha-ha!"

"What is that huge nose?"

"Ha-ha."

"A trunk with a butt."

Samantha gasps into a barely controlled sob. "Jack. Is it really bad? I made the nose too long. What can I —?"

"No. No, Sammy. It's really good. I was having a bit of fun with you before. It's a fantastic dog. Winger's just being … hmmm, Winger." I shout back to him: "Get lost. You couldn't make something as good as this."

"As if. Oooooh," Winger howls in a whiny voice. His mates sing along.

I snap at him. "Cut it out —"

From out of nowhere the bald head of our teacher, Mr. Angelou, appears, shining in the sun. Right away Winger shuts up. I give Winger a don't-mess-around-with-me look, while Mr. Angelou tells him off. He stands there like a stuffed scarecrow. His mates disappear of course. I race up to the library with Samantha tagging behind me.

The librarian, Mrs. Lopez, likes me. I helped her stack and sort hundreds of books last year. Spent a lot of time in the library at lunchtime. I don't know how I'd have made it without the library. Good place to go when the playground goes feral. "Hello, Jack. Haven't seen you for a while." Her voice sings like always. I think it's because of her Spanish accent.

"I've started playing rugby. I'm in the reserves. Practice at lunchtime."

"But the library's still here," she sings. "I've got some interesting new space photos. From NASA."

"Sounds great. I'll check them out Monday."

She smiles at Samantha. "That project looks very good. Put it over there with the other models."

Samantha pushes her hand through my arm. Embarrassing. "Thanks, Jack," she whispers.

I shove her hand away, check that no one's seen and escape just as the bell rings. Jumping two stairs at a time, I run into the school yard and catch up with Paul. He flicks his rugby ball at me. "Practice today, Jack. See how good you are at a real game."

Laughing, I flick it back. "Still like soccer."

"You're kidding. Rugby rules."

Everyone piles into class. I head for my desk, next to Christopher. He points to a paper bag full of cookies from his parents' Vietnamese bakery. "For Nanna."

I pretend to do a Nanna wobble, then slump into my chair. "Lucky for Nanna you're my best mate."

I look over at Anna. She grins at me as she gets out her work. George Hamel walks in. A few girls ogle him and giggle. I roll my eyes. What's he got? OK, he's captain of the 13A team. Plays great rugby, but what else? Yeah, maybe he's tall, got muscles, even if they're coming out of his head. Ha-ha. OK, he looks all right, but so do a lot of guys. He's still not great at reading. George Hamel winks at Becky and Jasmin, who titter at him. Those girls need a brain. One between two would be good. They're messaging under the desk. George Hamel looks at Anna, but she ignores him and gives me one of her huge smiles. George has got to know by now that she's not interested in him.

I give him a look. He shrugs and smirks as if to say, It's always worth a try. He saunters to his desk.

Classes seem so long today. It's Friday. Mum's having a barbecue this weekend. I stare out of the window. A sea eagle glides in the breeze, going out towards the ocean. Grandad and I always stopped to watch a sea eagle. He'd say, "We all have wings like eagles. You can soar, Jack. Be anything you want to be."

Christopher kicks me under the desk and adjusts his new black glasses. "Hey, why did you do ...?" I start to say, then I see Mr. Angelou walking down the aisle. Christopher slides his work over my way and I pretend to be working on it with him.

Lunchtime at last. Paul and I grab our rugby cleats. Paul laughs. "What's it like playing the *right* game?"

"Funny, Paul. Let's go."

Anna and her best girlfriend, Maggie, take their lunches and walk with us across the school yard to the sports fields. Becky and her friends are hanging around George Hamel, watching him run up and down the field with the other 13A rugby guys. Anna shakes her head.

"I've got better things to do than watch those boys sweating and panting. Showing off."

"Hey, that'll be me in a minute." I pretend to run in slow motion. "Anna, don't you want to watch us? Paul reckons he's pretty good." Paul knuckles my arm. "Owwwh."

Anna slips her arm through Maggie's and gives a cheeky smile. "I'll watch you when you're doing more than showing off. When you play a game." They giggle as they stroll away to join some girls eating lunch under a tree.

I stand there watching her until Paul nudges me. "Anna's really cute."

Red starts creeping up my face. "If you say so." I roll my eyes.

Paul cracks up. "I'd say *you* say so."

"Yeah, right. Come on. See who gets to the field first." I bolt ahead. Paul bolts after me.

End of day bell rings. Christopher and I are walking across the school yard. We nearly get knocked over by some guys running to the car pickup. Christopher's glasses fall off. Winger calls out, "What are ya? Blind? Slanty eyes. Four eyes."

I shout at Winger, "Hey, cut it out."

Christopher checks out his glasses, then puts them back on, relieved. "They're not broken."

"That Winger's an idiot."

Sammy and Anna are in the bus line saving a place for us. They wave us over.

I get into line next to Anna. "How'd your project go, Sammy?" I just control a laugh.

Samantha's very touchy about it. "Everyone liked it, but Mrs. Lopez thought I could cut a bit off the dog's nose." She flicks her ponytail at me. "So I did it at lunchtime in the library. But not because it looked like an elephant or anything."

I'm dying to make a joke, then notice Anna's cannonball eyes. I have second thoughts. "Yeah. Yeaaah … Your dog never looked anything like an … elephant."

At the front of the bus line, George Hamel and Winger are expertly chucking a ball between them. Need a lot of practice to get as good as them. Becky and Jasmin are still hanging around them. Boring. Becky flicks her red hair and bleats, "You're so good at passing the ball, George."

Anna gives an I-don't-believe-them look. George Hamel puts the ball under one arm, smiles coolly, points a finger at the girls. He cocks his thumb, mouths "pow." Becky takes a photo on her phone. They giggle as Jasmin sends the Hamel "pow" flick to friends. I want to make a joke, but I've learned something. Some people can't take a joke too well. George Hamel's one of those.

"Bus," Samantha yaps. Wow, she's beginning to sound like Puppy.

George Hamel, Winger and their mates Becky and Jasmin laugh and shove each other up the bus steps. They'll tumble into the last seats as usual. Good — far away from us.

As I get on, I spot four seats in the middle and turn to tell Anna. "Over there."

Anna smiles. She's got this special smile that makes her eyes smile too.

"Get moving, Romeo."

I twist around. It's grump bus driver Len. He's been driving buses too long if you ask me. His gray shirt is open and his gray pants have coffee stains. He looks at me, then Anna, then me. Then Anna. Len's gravelly voice is like fingernails down my eardrum. "Get moving, lover boy. Haven't got all day."

There are laughs from around the bus. Anna blushes and can't even look at me. My stomach knots. I take a breath, stand straight and look seriously into Len's eyes. "Your fly's open." I push Anna ahead, give a shove to Samantha. Christopher takes the hint. We head down the aisle.

"What the …?" Len calls after me. "Hey." I turn back, still making for my seat. Kids are still jostling onto the bus from the front. He has to turn around.

"Get moving." He barks at them, turns back to look at me again, then grins.

There're a few pats on my back. Anna whispers in my ear. "You're funny." She touches my arm. "You stood up to him."

I guess I did. I smile, until I see Becky on the backseat. Groan. Becky is hanging next to George Hamel. Jasmin is next to Winger. I quickly get to the empty seats and turn my back on them. Samantha slides into the seat, then Anna. Christopher shoves into the seat behind them, then me.

"Hey, the barbecue's at my place on Sunday. You all coming?"

Anna beams. "Can't wait."

Everyone'll be there. Anna's making a mango cake. Her parents are bringing a special salad with olives. Anna loves black olives. I wouldn't say I love them. I'm getting used to them.

"Mum and Dad are baking buns. Lots of them. Nanna's going to be pretty happy." Christopher nudges me. "Nanna comes around a lot to the bakery. Mum always gives her a cream bun or iced doughnut or a cookie."

I laugh. "That's Nanna."

"Yeah. Mum likes her visiting. Nanna always brings Mum something."

"Like underpants and socks? Ha-ha."

"Only once." Christopher adjusts his glasses, swallowing a laugh. "Matching socks and underpants. They were purple."

I splutter. "Did they glow in the dark?"

Smiling, Christopher nods. Samantha giggles.

Anna bursts out laughing. "She bought some for my parents too."

Chapter 3

Riding the Wave

Rob's standing next to the yellow van in his board shorts and sunglasses with white zinc cream on his nose. Our surfboards are on the roof rack. The sun's shining, the sky is blue, the wind's blowing just right. I'm racing to the car when Mum flounces out holding a dish towel on her hip.

"Where are you boys off to?"

Mum knows where we're off to. "Back soon, Mum," I yell out.

"Stop, Jack." I turn around. "The shed. It's got to be cleared before the barbecue."

"Why? No one's going into the shed, except for

Rob. It's *our* workplace. And the barbecue's tomorrow anyway."

"That's right. Tomorrow. When there's no time."

"But Mum … the surf's —"

"You have to get rid of those dead experiments, Jack."

"Mum, they're not dead —"

"They smell like they are."

Rob scratches his prickly head. "What about a surf first?"

Mum gets this disappointed look. "What's that teaching Jack?"

"That guys can do two things in one day, babe."

"Yes, clear the shed, then surf, Rob." Nanna waddles out at this exact moment. So both Mum and Nanna are staring at Rob. "And I need to get out all the garden chairs and set them up. They're right at the back of the shed."

Rob nudges me. "Come on, mate. We won't win this battle. When Mum and Nanna are on a clean-and-organize mission, they take no survivors."

"Rob." Mum's hair bobs and her face goes pink. "I'm not like that. I thought you'd want to help."

"Come on, babe. I do. Just joking. Let's get on with it, Jack." He nods at Mum. "Jack and me, we've got serious shed work to do."

"Hey, Rob, surf later?"

"For sure. Let's get this shed done fast."

I put on some surfing music and we get to work. Rob's dragging garden chairs from behind a pile of surfing gear. I check out my Pontos. Failed experiments are chucked in the trash. Then I sort and organize, label and line up my experiments. Looks pretty good. Now, for my workbench. I sort beakers, Bunsen burners, jars on the shelves. Throw out broken junk. Stack my *New Scientist* magazines in a pile on the floor. I check out an article: "Arctic melt will spark weird weather." "Hey, Rob, we could have a really boiling summer." I flash *New Scientist* at him.

"Hey, you could have a really boiling mum if we don't get this done."

"Funny." I throw empty boxes and old computer parts in the trash.

Rob calls out, "Hey, there's two barbecues here. There's a big one. Oh, but it looks pretty old. I'll get it working."

"That's great, Rob." I'm not listening as I check out my tool pegboard hooked to the wall. Stuck at the top is Albert Einstein's quote. *Anyone who has never made a mistake has never tried anything new.*

I've made plenty of mistakes, that's for sure.

Hooks have fallen off my board. I put them back in and reorganize my tools into sections: hammers, screwdrivers, saws, wrenches. Grandad's old metal toolbox is on the floor. I crouch down and check what's inside. Good stuff. Then I see it. A ring wrench. The twelve-point one. My throat goes dry as I pick it up. The wrench …

I was nearly eight. That day I was working with Grandad on the car in the driveway with its hood up. Grandad was wearing his blue-flannel checked shirt and khaki work pants. He'd found the problem. He said I was his "right-hand man." We were a team and we could depend on each other. I liked that. Grandad called out to me. "Ring wrench. The twelve-point one."

I got the set of wrenches from his toolbox. I hoped I'd found the right one. I held my breath. "Here it is, Grandad."

Grandad coughed hard as he took it. "You're pretty good, mate." He smiled. Suddenly he clasped his chest. His glasses fell to the ground and then he fell down, dragging the box of wrenches with him. The crash was so loud.

"What's wrong? Grandad, get up. Get up. Get up."

I crouched beside him, holding his head in my arms. He gasped. "Get Nanna. Mum. Go, Jack. Go."

I ran for my life inside the house, shouting, screaming. "Mum, Nanna, Mum. Come on. Come on. It's Grandad. Grandad."

Mum and Nanna ran out. Grandad opened his eyes and he reached out for my hand. I held it as hard as I could.

Rob shouts. "Hey, Jack, can you give us a hand taking this old barbecue out? Just help me move it to under the awning."

I jump, dropping the wrench. It clangs to the floor. "Oh yeah, sure." I pick it up, hold it for a while, then carefully hang it on the pegboard.

The barbecue is out. The garden chairs are in the backyard. The shed is organized. Rob and I look around. "It's done, Jack."

"Hey, Rob, let's surf."

"Yeah, let's get goin'."

Mum waves from the kitchen window, singing, "Love you." Nanna's head pops up next to her. She can't stand missing out on anything. Samantha runs through the door with Ollie in front and Puppy behind.

Rob parks his van in the parking lot on the cliff overlooking the beach. We stand there watching the surf for a long while. The ocean seems endless. I look up hoping for a sea eagle. "Hey, Jack." Rob points to a surf break. I turn to watch a wave crash on the headland. George Hamel is sitting on his board out there with some girls and guys, waiting for the next set of waves.

Out of nowhere, a lump sticks in my throat. George Hamel. A flash of him shoving me at the bus stop. Yelling. Snarling. I close my eyes tight. Take a deep breath. Another one. Feel scared.

I shake my head. *No.* That's never going to happen again.

"Are you okay, Jack?"

I nod at Rob. "Yeah. Let's go. Surf's up."

We carry our boards down the cliff path to the beach. Becky and Jasmin are lying on the sand covered in oil. Haven't they ever heard of skin cancer? They ignore me as I head for the surf with Rob. I run into the waves, splashing water behind me. Jumping onto my board, I paddle out just beyond the break. Rob paddles beside me.

George Hamel sees me. We nod at each other.

Rob and I watch the swell. I gaze up and it's like an electric charge. The sea eagle is there. Its wings are huge and its underbelly is white. Grandad. Grandad. I stretch out my hand and the eagle swerves towards me. Then it's gone.

"Jack," Rob calls out to me, and points to the swell.

I give him the thumbs-up. I turn my board towards the shore and paddle hard into the wave. Catching it, I push up, stand, edge into position. The feeling of the wind and surf, the wall of water peeling behind me, and the power of the sea are incredible. I ride the wave right into shore.

Chapter 4

The World's Greatest Cook

Sunday morning. Just finished my paper route. "Breakfast," I shout, as I run past Rob working on the old barbecue. I nearly fall over my feet when I see his hat and matching apron — *The World's Greatest Cook.*

"Good one, Rob." I jump backward up the back step, pointing at his apron.

He laughs. "Yeah, that's me. Greatest Cook."

I grab a cereal bowl from the kitchen cupboard. No bacon and eggs this morning. Mum's too busy. She's tapping her feet as she prepares salads. She sings to me in tune with The Beatles: "*Help, you need some juice. Help, not just any juice. Help yourself. It's in the fridge. Help, freshly squeezed by me.*"

Grinning, I put my hands over my ears. "Mum, stop singing. My head." I switch on the radio.

Mum just laughs. Then Samantha laughs, rocking in time as she arranges sunflowers in a really tall vase. She's dropped one on the floor. I grab my camera and click Mum singing, Samantha rocking and Puppy in a serious battle with the sunflower. I'm pretty sure the sunflower's the one screaming "Help!"

With my bowl of cereal, I plonk myself down at the kitchen table next to Nanna. Puss is in her lap. She looks up and smiles at me. "Nanna, are you seriously rolling Christmas paper napkins?" She nods proudly. "But it's not Christmas."

"I got them at a bargain price and they're excellent quality."

"There's a *huge* red Santa Claus on them."

She grins. "I know." She smacks her gums together, then puts in her teeth.

Samantha looks up from the sunflowers and groans. "Your teeth … don't, Nanna, please …"

Nanna taps her teeth. Smiles cheekily. "Need my teeth." With that, she takes a huge bite from a raisin bun. The raisins are sticking between her chompers.

"That's awful, Nanna." She doesn't care. I focus my camera. "Smile." She gives a big toothy grin. "That'll look good on my Facebook."

There's a sudden explosion. I splutter cereal all over Nanna's Christmas napkins. Mum drops the salad bowl. Nanna's mouth opens in shock. I race to the window. It's Rob and the barbecue. His face is as red as his hibiscus Hawaiian shirt. I race outside and shout back to everyone, "Keep out of the way."

"What's happening, Jack?" Mum's at the window.

I wave. "Just stay there."

Rob calls out. "Stay put. Just getting this working." There are a few more explosions. Rob jumps back. I'm doubled over laughing. Got to film this. "Cut it out, Jack. This'll work."

"Not having much luck." I'm filming. The barbecue splutters and burps.

Rob's head looks like a pink cactus. His face is scrunched. He's determined. He strikes a match. Oh no. This is going to be a disaster. "Well, this'll either light the thing or take out half the suburb. Move back, Jack."

The bang is major. Smoke pumps out of the barbecue. Flames shoot up like arrows. Rob's coughing and choking. Mum hurries to the back porch with Samantha behind her. I charge between them, racing into the kitchen. "Mum, Sammy. Get out of the way." I snatch the fire blanket off the wall, pull off the red bag and sprint back outside towards the fire. Fully opening the white fire blanket, I yell, "Rob, stand back."

"It's under control, Jack," Rob splutters.

"Rob. Just get out of my way." He stumbles backward. I fling the blanket over the fire. The fire doesn't like it and throws out some spits and hisses. Then the flames slowly die down, with smoke drifting through them.

Mum's clapping. "Wonderful, darling." Samantha's clapping too.

Nanna points at Rob, chuckling. *"The World's Greatest Cook."*

Everyone bursts out laughing, even Rob. "OK, it's funny. Very funny. You can all leave now. I'm going to get this barbecue to work if it kills me. Go inside. Right. Go. Go."

We tumble back into the kitchen, still laughing. Mum eventually stops giggling in between buttering rolls. I reckon Samantha's making another dog-elephant model as she piles the buttered rolls into a basket, lining them up into a trunk. Nanna goes back to rolling those napkins at the table. Wow, she must have bought thousands. I fill the cooler with ice. I look out of the window at Rob and the barbecue. I call out to Mum, "Looks like the old barbecue's working now."

"It's good to see that it's still useful." Mum stops with the butter knife in midair, like she's trying to remember. "It's been in the shed for years. The last time …" Mum's voice peters out.

Samantha pipes up. "When? I can't remember."

Mum goes a bit pale as she looks at Samantha. "You were nearly four, darling."

Samantha stops and gives Mum a strange stare. "Mum, was it …?"

Mum's eyes start watering. "Yes. It was your father's," she whispers. "It's been a long time."

She looks at Sammy and me. "Time we used the barbecue again."

"I barely remember him, Mum." Samantha's voice trembles.

Mum takes her hand. "That's his loss, darling."

Samantha presses her lips together. "Rob will cook up a great barbecue."

"Yes, he will." Mum looks at her. Then at me.

I get this lump in my throat. I remember Dad. I walk to the window. I remember the barbecue now. Why did Mum keep it? Rob shouldn't be using it. Maybe my dad will come back. Maybe he'll want to use it? Maybe I should find him? Tell him that we've still got his barbecue? Through the window, I see Rob's chef's hat bobbing up and down. He's checking knobs and scratching his head. I try not to laugh. When he sees me, his face breaks into a grin. Rob waves a pair of tongs in the air and yells out, "It's workin', Jack. It's all good."

I swallow. "Yeah, Mum. We'll have a great barbecue."

Chapter 5

Hot Sausages!

Rob blowing up the barbecue was something. I bend over my desk and upload the video clip and post it on Facebook. Too funny.

I check out Ponto on my windowsill. It's Ponto Number 39 and growing really well. I cross my fingers that this one works. I take a few photos of it. Put down my camera and do some work on my soundboard. *Ping. Ping.* I look at my screen and hoot. Rob and the barbecue.

Comments:

Paulo: Im so boooored doing homewk. Hey, Worlds WORST cook!

Christopher: Whoooooahhhh!!!!! Rob's on fire.

Anna: What happened? C ya soon.
Likes: 4. Shares: 3.

"C ya soon?" I look at the time and scramble to my closet. Anna's going to be here any minute. I drag on my jeans. Get out my T-shirt. Anna'll like this one for sure. Splashed across it is *We are all star stuff — Carl Sagan.* I drag it over my head. Socks. I sniff them. Clean. Phew. Pull them on, then shove my feet into my shoes.

The doorbell rings. The Napolis' voices echo down the hall. I check myself in the mirror. Flick my hair back. It's not too bad. OK. I sprint down the hallway. Mrs. Napoli is handing Mum a gigantic salad platter with lots of olives. Mr. Napoli puts his arms around Mum and gives her a whopping Italian double-cheek kiss.

Anna's standing behind them holding a mango cake. I catch my breath. She looks really amazing, wearing a green-and-yellow flowery dress with a golden ribbon through her hair. Anna smiles at me. She flicks her head so that her dark hair swirls. "Hi, Jack."

"Hi, Anna." My face goes hot.

Anna laughs and kisses each of my cheeks. From the corner of my eye, I see Mum with a know-it-all smile. My face gets hotter.

I growl under my breath, "Can you stop, Mum?"

Lucky for me, just at that second, Christopher's parents appear at the door with baskets of bread and cakes. Mum's distracted. "Wonderful to see you. You shouldn't have brought so much."

Christopher and I slap hands. "Let's get out of here."

Anna stamps her foot, then raises her hand. "What about me? Or is it only for the boys?"

"Only for the boys." I wink at her and lift my arm. She thinks it's hilarious and we slap hands. Then Christopher does the same and the three of us head out through the backyard to the park just past the back fence.

The clouds are white ribbons across the sky. The sun's shining and the cricket game is on. Christopher and I are fielding. Mum's bowling, except she can't bowl. Rob's trying to help Mum. Wish him luck there. Samantha is cheering. She really knows how to cheer. Loudly. My eardrums are going to burst. Mr. Tran is batting, except he can't bat. Nanna is keeping score. So at least someone can do something right.

Mum bowls a weak throw to Mr. Tran who hits the ball up into the sky.

Nanna throw her hands in the air and calls out. "Six."

The ball sails out over the field into the bush.

Christopher waves to his dad. "Shot, Dad."

"Six and out, mate. House rules." Rob raises his hands.

Mr. Tran accepts it. "Ahhhh ... OK."

It's Anna's turn. She takes the bat from Mr. Tran and gets into place. Her face is scrunched and the wind catches her curls. She waits for Mum to bowl.

"Go, Anna," I call out.

Anna's face lights up as she turns to look at me.

Mum sings back, laughing. "She's on the wrong team, Jack."

"The wrong team, Jack. Ha-ha."

"Shut up, Christopher. Can we watch the game?"

Mum's rainbow skirt flips up and her hair fuzzes into a ball as she runs with her arm raised. She throws the ball. Anna swings, thumping out a huge lollipop hit. The ball sails through the air and I run towards it. "Got it. Got it." Getting into position, I eye the ball's arc. It's going to land right in my hands like a fat plum falling off a tree. Wow, Mum so can't bowl. Screams belt out from the field. "Go, Jack. Go, Jack. Catch it."

Like in slow motion the ball heads for me. My arms are out. I glance at Anna racing as fast as she can to get runs. The palms of my hands open, the ball touches my hands. I fumble, letting it slip through my fingers. Groans and laughs come from everywhere.

"Ohhhh ... Just missed that." I bend down to pick up the ball and sneak a look at Anna.

She's beaming. It was worth it.

Cricket's over and no one's sure who won. In the end, Nanna was hopeless at keeping score. Too busy talking to Mrs. Tran about how to bake buns. Who cares? Starving Jack. It's barbecue time.

I can't believe it. Rob's still wearing his *The World's Greatest Cook* hat. I give him a you've-got-to-be-kidding look. He nods towards Mum. Oh, that's right. She bought it for him. And the matching apron. He's *got* to wear it. "Lookin' good, Rob."

"I'm a good-lookin' bloke." Rob rubs his prickly head and nearly knocks off his hat. He chuckles and flips the sausages with the tongs. "They're gunna be perfect."

Christopher, Mr. Tran and Mr. Napoli are standing together talking, holding their drinks. There's growly yapping going on. Everyone looks around. Anna and Samantha are chasing Puppy, who's chasing his tail. I call out, "Puppy's gunna catch that tail. That'll be the end of the story. Ha-ha."

Christopher laughs. "That's funny, Jack."

"I'm a funny guy."

Rob's in the middle of demonstrating to Mr. Napoli how he put a new clutch in his van. I sniff and look down. Wisps of black smoke pump from the barbecue. I nudge Rob. "Perfect?"

He looks down. "Yipes." He grabs the tongs.

I shout. "Burned sausages ready. Come and get them."

Chapter 6

Red Socks

I hear Nanna in the bathroom. She had a lot of cookies and cream buns. I bet she has a stomach-ache. She said that she would just have one more bun. Just one more. She really can't control herself. I like that her room is at the end of the hallway, overlooking the garden. She watches me when I'm working on my experiments outside. She gets a cup of tea, a cookie, a book, but she looks out to see what's happening. I wave to her and she waves back.

I peer through my telescope. The moon is a little bigger tonight. There's so much out there we can't see. So much *here* we can't see. Today was a great day.

I start chuckling at the hopeless joke Christopher told me on the cricket field.

"Why are Trans so useful? They Trans-fix!"

He's smart and he'll become a doctor and save the world, but he sure can't tell jokes. The Trans don't tell many jokes. Maybe because they work really hard in their bakery to make up for everything in Vietnam. The war. Leaving their family there. Escaping in an old wooden boat. Christopher was happy his parents took time off and came to the barbecue today. Me too.

I look at my photo wall. There's Christopher and me with our Vietnam project. Mr. Angelo made everyone do the project — on where our families came from and who we are. I didn't know about Christopher's family before. Grandad fought in the Vietnam War. Christopher's family lived through it, escaped and are here, safe. We're best mates now. Mum took the photo. It's actually in focus, which is a miracle. I stare at Grandad's medals on my wall. He's a hero. Saved a soldier's life. A shiver runs down my back. Nanna made me take the medals. "But I'm not a hero," I told her. She said Grandad wanted me to have them.

Ping. Ping. My phone. Message.

Anna: Did U drop the ball on purpose?

I message back.

Jack: Sun was in my eyes. U did a great hit.

Anna messages back.

Anna: Had fun.

Me too. The sun gets in my eyes. I check out Anna's photo on the wall. "At least when she's around. Did I say that out loud, Hector?" I give Hector a few cookie crumbs. "Promise not to tell."

The school bus is packed and everyone's wearing red. Red streamers, red T-shirts, red armbands. Red temporary tattoos on arms and legs. Becky's got *George Hamel* written in red marker up her leg. She's a dope. I'm wearing red socks. It's the big game today. Our school, Boat Harbour, against the enemy — Forrest Lodge. I wave at Christopher as he gets on. He's stuck at the front of the bus. He tries to move towards us. Some idiot blocks him. "Stay put, four eyes." Yeah, it's Winger of course.

I yell out to Christopher. "I'm here." He waves, wedged between kids.

Anna's hair is a mass of red ribbons. She looks up and smiles. I smile back and feel my face go hot. Everyone's stuck between kids. I look out of the window as the bus bumps along the cliffs. I never get sick of looking at the ocean.

The bus pulls up. A red army of kids piles off. Christopher and Anna wait for me. We rattle into the school yard together, with Samantha following.

Paul bounds up. "Hey, guys. Big game today." He passes his rugby ball between his hands.

Mr. Angelou's voice comes over the PA system. "Everyone to the hall for assembly. Quietly and quickly, please."

Mrs. Lopez hurries down from the library with red ribbons around her wrists. All the teachers will be at the game today.

There's laughing, shoving, running as we pile into the hall. Paul thumps to the front with the rest of his team. I see George Hamel give him a high five. They're on the same team, but I sort of wish they weren't. Paul's my mate, not his. George Hamel doesn't notice me. All of a sudden, I get this sick feeling inside. Flashes of George chasing me last year, yelling at me, shoot through my head. I grit my teeth and look at Christopher who's right beside me. I'm not letting George Hamel, Winger or anyone make me feel like nothing ever again. Smiling, I pretend to punch Christopher in the arm. "Hey, like your red socks."

He laughs. "Yeah, great minds think alike."

We tumble into our seats. Anna sits on my right side with Maggie next to her. Christopher's on my left. Principal Brown is on the stage. The hall quiets. He welcomes everyone then motions for us all to get up. "Everyone stand for the school song." The music starts and we sing. Principal Brown nods. "Well done." He mustn't have heard me: I sound like a frog. He directs Mr. Angelou onto the stage.

Mr. Angelou motions to everyone to sit. Then he nods at George Hamel and the rugby team and climbs the stage steps. He looks like an overfed giant, with his bald head shining. His voice booms through the hall. "Today is the big game. You all look great in school colors. I don't know who'll win this game, but Boat Harbour will win if we all show school spirit and do our best." He looks down at the front row of rugby players and gestures for them to stand. They all get up, turn around and wave. "Let's give it up for our champion team." Mr. Angelou applauds and everyone else joins in. He points to George Hamel. "Now for the captain of the 13As. George Hamel, come on up."

George Hamel charges up the steps and everyone claps. I slow clap and slide a look at Anna. She's finger clapping. Mr. Angelou gives him the microphone, then stands back.

"Thanks, everyone. We'll do our best." He throws his arm into the air. "Go Reds. Go Boat Harbour."

The audience hoots and whistles. George waves everyone down. The hall quiets. "This is gunna be a great game." He lifts his arms over his head, then pumps his fists. The other players follow him. The

assembly does too, cheering and waving.

Mr. Angelou's voice booms across the stage. "Settle down. Settle down." He points to the front row. "Stand up, boys. Winger. Hawkie. Paul. All of you. Stand, boys. Turn around." They get up and face the crowd.

George looks at the audience. "We're gunna win this." He raises one arm and yells. "Yeahhh."

The assembly erupts. Winger belts the air. Hawkie copies him. The others follow. George Hamel's voice blasts over the mic. "Come on, Boat Harbour."

More yelling. George holds out his arm to Principal Brown and Mr. Angelou, who nod. George waves to the audience. "Thanks. I mean it. Thanks, everyone." He winks at Becky, who shrieks. The hall fills with shouts, whistles and stamping feet.

I don't stamp my feet even though George Hamel is a great rugby player. Even though the hall is full of everyone else's cheers. I can't forget. Last year.

It was bad. I still don't get how it happened. Why it happened. Why I couldn't stop it. Why kids did it. Why my friends weren't friends anymore. Then there's the pool. I shudder. I don't get how people could do that to anyone. Corner, trap, hunt. Like I'm a bug to be squashed. Bullying. And I still don't get why it was me. George Hamel got caught in the end. So did his mates. Suspended from school. George won't do it again to me or anyone. I won't let it happen again. But I can't cheer.

These days George Hamel says hello to me in the corridors and in the playground. I say hello to him as well, but we're not mates. Not after what happened at the pool. Since then, Mr. Angelou keeps an eye on him, but today everyone's forgotten because he's the captain of the rugby team. The hero.

Anna puts her hand on my arm. I jump. Her eyes look worried. She mouths, "Are you OK?"

Anna hasn't forgotten. A true friend.

I take a breath. "Sure."

George Hamel gives the audience the thumbs-up. The clapping goes on and on as he walks off the stage.

As we head out of the hall to class, Mr. Angelou calls me over. "Are you OK to take photos at the game today? Do some filming as well?"

"Yeah, OK."

"I can always depend on you, Jack."

Chapter 7

Game's On

The stands are insane with screams. Rows of Forrest Lodge kids are a mass of blue with blue streamers, hats, signs — *WIN BLUES. Go, Blue, Go. BEAST Blues.* Rows of Boat Harbour kids are a mass of red with red streamers, hats, signs — *Reds Rulz. Hamel's a Legend, BOAT HARBOUR ROCKS!* Teachers march along the aisles checking that everyone is sitting and not being idiots. *Click. Click. Click.*

Players line up. The coaches huddle with their teams giving last-minute moves. Mr. Angelou is the referee. I'm on the sidelines. Mr. Angelou nods at me. "OK, Jack?" I hold up my camera and nod. I'm filming this. Christopher tries to look useful and carries my camera case, but we're really just hanging together. He's got his black glasses tied on with rubber bands, just in case he gets knocked. "Glasses, Christopher." I roll my eyes. "Nerd alert."

He shrugs. "You're right, but I can't get them broken."

I laugh. "Loser."

He smiles. "Yep, that's me."

"Ready to run? You've got to keep up with me. Right?"

"Right." He pats his rubber bands. "And ready."

Mr. Angelou blows the whistle and it's on. George Hamel charges down the field, handling the ball with real know-how, out in front of his team. There's a roar from the Reds — "Boat Harbour. Boat Harbour. Go, George. Beast. Beast. Beast." The Blue's center intercepts and there's a roar from the Blues — "Forrest Lodge. Forrest Lodge. Go, Legend. Go."

I focus my lens into the stands, filming yells, faces exploding, kids jumping up and waving hands. Becky's long red hair flies in the wind as she throws her arms in the air. Jasmin's screaming next to her. I stop on Anna, who's calling out, "Reds! Reds! Reds!" Maggie's jumping all over her. There's a huge shout from the stands. I turn my camera to the game. Winger has the ball. He's lightning fast, belting down the field, outstripping the Blues. Then it's Paul. He takes a pass and runs. He's down, tackled by a huge guy, the ball knocked out of his hands.

Mr. Angelou blows the whistle. There's a scrum. Paul's catching his breath. I crouch at the sidelines. Focus my lens deep into the clump of guys. Paul looks around, nods at Mr. Angelou, then he throws the ball into the scrum.

Legs, arms, spikes, kicks. I film shots of a hand yanking an ear, nearly pulling it off. Spikes dig into legs and there're screams. George Hamel's hand grabs hard into a thigh. Winger's face drips sweat as he belts players. Hawkie's in his way, pressing against him. Winger growls and jabs back his elbow. George Hamel tries to grab Winger's arm. Too late. Winger's elbow slams against Hawkie's face. Hawkie falls to the ground, groaning. His nose's covered in blood. It looks broken. I film. Then take stills. *Click. Click. Click.*

Mr. Angelou blows the whistle hard. The game stops. Reds and Blues look at each other, stand up, grazed knees, mud on faces, hands on hips, taking the chance to catch a breath. George Hamel grabs Winger. Away from Mr. Angelou and forgetting about me, he says, "Whatcha do? Hawkie's our man."

"Nothin'."

Coach quickly checks out Hawkie, the old man's cauliflower ears and bent nose close to Hawkie's face. He sprays water on Hawkie's bloody nose.

"It hurts, Coach."

Coach's face is blotchy purple. "You're all right. Man up, Hawkie. Are you a hawk? Or a chicken?" Coach waves to some guys to help Hawkie off the field. Christopher and I watch. I get this sick, angry feeling inside. I rumble to Christopher, "Coach is a birdbrain. No. That's insulting to birds. He's got no brain."

"Some people never change." Christopher turns to look at the old man.

"Maybe you're right." I click Coach's face: pink and angry. Coach calls George Hamel over. They talk. Coach motions a reserve to get onto the field then shouts to Mr. Angelou. "Hawkie's fine." I turn my camera on Hawkie. He's not fine. What am I supposed to do?

Mr. Angelou waves. Blows his whistle. Game's on again. It's fast and furious. Score is 18–16 to the Blues. Halftime. Guys are gulping down water, huddled with their coaches.

George Hamel eyes his team, thrusts out his arm. "Come on, guys. We can do this. Right?"

The team slap hands. "Right." "Right." "Right."

Second half. The Reds run onto the field. The Blues run on too. The whistle. Tries, runs, scrums. Crowd yells. "Go, George. Smash 'em."

Coach races along the sidelines, shouting. "Winger: throw. George: now. Now! Kill 'em. Kill 'em."

George Hamel has the ball now. He barges through the opposing backs, dives for the line, slams the ball right down between the posts. Winner. Score 32–28. Boat Harbour explodes in the stands, cheering and shouting. "Hamel! Hamel! Hamel!"

Hamel and Winger leap into the air, slapping hands together. *Click*. Mr. Angelou's jumping in the air with his hands out. *Click*. I pan the fields. Blues leaning on each other. *Click*. Reds crazy with winning. *Click*. I jump back to Coach's face. His mouth's wide open, his teeth exposed and tongue stuffed back against his throat in an ear-piercing shout. *Click, click, click.*

Chapter 8

Legends

I'm uploading the video and photos of the game on to my computer. Mr. Angelou wants to see the photos tomorrow. Some of them … I don't know if I can show him. *Ping. Ping.* Check my phone. Photos from kids at the game flash up on the screen: George Hamel sliding over the line. Winger sprinting with the ball. Reds and Blues on the field. Kids cheering. Facebook messages keep pinging:

Anna: Great game.
Hotchic1: Hamel's a legend.
Hotchic2: Winger's a legend.
That's got to be Becky and Jasmin. So stupid.

Paulo: Only game to play! Ha!
Eagle: Beast! Beast! Beast!
Christopher: Can't wait to c yr photos.

Christopher didn't see what I saw through my camera lens. Inside the scrum. Don't want to get him involved. Just got to think what to do.

I hear the back door slam. Rob yells down the hallway. "How'd the game go?"

"Great," I yell from my bedroom. I'm not in the mood for Rob or anyone.

"Who won?"

"Boat Harbour," I yell again and close my door.

Rob's knocking at my door. What's wrong with him? Can't he see I don't want to talk? "Hey, Jack. Got something for you."

I stick my head out of my door and nearly crash into him. Rob's holding up a jar covered with suction pads. "They just came in at work. Thought they'd be good for your experiments. I've got a box of them. Come and see."

I slouch down the hallway. He hands me the jar and I check it out.

"What do ya think?"

I shake my head. I'm thinking about that scrum. Coach. Winger. But Rob's just waiting. Got to say something. I turn the jar. "Yeah, Rob. It's a bit like the world." I wait a second. "If it didn't suck, we'd all fall off." Rob scratches his prickly head. I try to explain. "Suck. You know, like life can suck. Like gravity keeps us stuck here? Sucking us onto the world. We'd fall off otherwise. Like the jar has suckers on it. Get it?"

Lightbulb moment. Rob gets it and laughs. Mum looks up from cooking and fluffs her hair. "Jack's so smart." Groan. Nanna doesn't even look up. Firstly she's half deaf and secondly she's too busy helping Sammy clean up another wee. Puppy needs to be toilet trained *soon*.

"I've got something for you girls too." Rob ducks out the back door to the porch. He strides back inside with three bunches of flowers. Long red roses for Mum. "For the best babe ever." I roll my eyes. Rob twirls Mum around as she holds the flowers close to her chest. "And for my other girls." Rob gives Samantha a bunch of baby-pink roses and some white jasmine to Nanna.

Samantha hugs Rob. "Thanks, Dad."

A creepy shiver runs down my spine. I wish I knew what a dad was. Where my dad was.

"They're lovely, Rob." Nanna sniffs the jasmine and waddles over to me so I can sniff too.

I smell the flowers. Can't help smiling at her toothy grin. Nanna does that to me. "Hey, Nanna, I'll get you a vase."

Love Nanna. She puts her hand over mine. Her hand's swollen, a bit twisty, but soft. "You're just like your grandad, Jack."

Hate Nanna saying that. I'm not as good as Grandad. I wish I was.

Next morning. School. Bell rings. "Jack." Mr. Angelou strides towards me. "I'm getting the newsletter together. Great game yesterday. Expect some brilliant shots from our number one school photographer. Can you show them to me at lunchtime?"

"Sure." Maybe not all of them. I don't know. Hate Mr. Angelou saying I'm the best photographer. I take photos, that's all.

"See you in class, Jack." He strides off to the staff room.

Christopher sits next to me in class.

There're calls across the desks.

"Great game."

"Boat Harbour showed those Forresters."

"Go, Winger."

"Best captain. George rulz."

I look around to the back. George Hamel and Winger are lapping it up. Hawkie's there with a bandaged nose. He sees me staring at him. Grinning stiffly, he taps his bandage, pretending he's fine.

"You OK?" I mouth. He gives a thumbs-up. I turn around. He's not OK. I'm not either. I've got to do something.

Mr. Angelou walks in carrying a pile of books. He's only with us half the time this year since he's been promoted to Executive Teacher. Mrs. Banneker is our other teacher. She likes science. We talk about space sometimes and what I see through my telescope. I showed her the NASA photos of the moon I got from the library. She's not sure if Ponto will feed the world, but, "It could," she says. I'd like that.

"Ethics today. That means you've got to think." Mr. Angelou taps the smart board. "Books are one of the best ways to understand events and people. Work out what you want the world to be. What you can do about it. We're going to start with ideas from one of the great classics of last century. *To Kill A Mockingbird.*" He holds up the book. At the same time "*To Kill A Mockingbird* by Harper Lee" flashes onto the board.

"Atticus Finch is a sole parent and the father of Scout, a girl who's nine and her brother, Jem, who's nearly thirteen. He gives his children great insights ..."

Mr. Angelou's voice fades into a murmur. I'm going to be thirteen soon, like Jem. Mum wants me to have a birthday party. "It's an important birthday.

You'll be a teenager," she says. We've got a mum. Jem and Scout have got a dad. It's the same, but not. I keep thinking about having a dad. Where he is. Not knowing is worse than Grandad dying. Grandad would have stayed if he could. My gut clamps into rock. I miss Grandad. But he didn't have a choice. Dad did.

Suddenly there's an elbow in my ribs. "Wake up," Christopher whispers. Mr. Angelou walks down the aisle. "Are you all paying attention?" Mr. Angelou stops still. "Atticus said that it's a sin to kill a mockingbird. Let's see what that means."

He points to George Hamel. "Read out that passage from the board." George stands up. He takes a breath, looks nervous. Starts reading.

"Mockingbirds don't do one thing except make music for us to enjoy. They don't eat up people's gardens, don't nest in corn cribs, they don't do one thing but sing their hearts out for us. That's why it's a sin to kill a mockingbird."

There are a few stumbles, but George reads it out. He looks relieved.

"Thanks, George. Good work."

Even though he's not my mate, yeah, it's good. Everyone needs to be able to read.

"A mockingbird? Do you know anyone like that?" Mr. Angelou waits. "Come on. Someone. Anyone?"

Dead silence. "All right. I'll tell you about one mockingbird I know. Jay. A big man with curly hair. Muscles like a wrestler. He cleaned in my mother's nursing home in the last few months of her life. My mother was trapped in a wheelchair. He'd sing to her instead of doing his work. My mother felt safe with him but the matron shouted at Jay. One day he didn't come in anymore. He lost his job. I call him a mockingbird." He looks around at the class. "What do you think? Is Jay a mockingbird?"

Anna's hand goes up. Mr. Angelou nods at her. "Yes, he's a mockingbird because he just wanted your mother to be happy and he didn't hurt anyone. And he lost his job. It's cruel."

"That's a great answer, Anna. Do you have a mockingbird you can talk about?"

Anna thinks for a moment. "I guess. Well, Princess Diana." There're a few laughs from the class. Anna's eyes go dark. Becky bleats like a sheep. For a change, Jasmin doesn't join in. Maybe because she loves anything "princess." Mr. Angelou looks around, but Becky stops quickly, especially since Jasmin isn't supporting her, so he nods at Anna to go on. "She helped homeless people, and kids with AIDS in Africa and she fought against land mines in war, so people wouldn't get blown up or lose their legs and … she was killed in a car crash." Anna stands up. "She was a mockingbird. And you don't kill them and you don't laugh."

"You're right." Mr. Angelou stares at a few kids tittering.

Anna stands there looking people in the eyes.

I call out. "Go, Anna." I start clapping. Christopher copies. Then Maggie does and her friends. Paul claps too and so does Mr. Angelou. Anna sits down. She flicks her hair and raises her chin at me.

"Thank you, Anna. Now everyone get out your notebooks. I want you to write down the name of one person who you think is a mockingbird. It can be personal or historical or a public figure or whoever you like. Explain why you feel that person is a mockingbird." He waits until everyone is ready. "Begin now."

I pick up my pen, stare into space, then slowly print, *Nanna*. I start writing. It's like my pen has a life of its own. Writing, writing, like it'll never stop.

Always there, just there. Not like my dad. And I know you're sad because Grandad's gone. I'm sad too, but you get on with everything and you're funny and help Mum and when Mum had cancer you were there. And you're always there for all of us. Always here for me. And you say you're grateful that you're allowed to live with us. I hate you being grateful because we're the lucky ones. Nanna, you're a mockingbird.

I'm not going to read this out to the class.

I wait for Mr. Angelou outside the staff room. "The photos, sir. I've edited and printed the good ones. What do you think of this one with George Hamel and Winger jumping in the air?"

"That's a great action shot. You've got natural timing, Jack."

I grin. "You might like this one too." I hand him the photo where Mr. Angelou's jumping up with his hands out. His eyes are bulging. He looks like an alien with the sun beaming off his bald head like a laser attack. It's *Star Trek* for sure. Just need to say, "Beam me up, Scotty."

Mr. Angelou stares at the photo for ages. "This is brilliant. This one is going above my desk now." He puts the other photos in his folder. "So what's happening about the film clip?"

"I'm editing it. I've been working on a soundboard and want to add some extra sound bites and special effects."

"Take your time. I've booked the computer lab for you to work on it next week. For your year's Project Strategy Day. I like the special project on sports and fairness that you've chosen to do for this term."

"Thanks, sir. Can Christopher do it with me? He's really smart with techy stuff."

"Good idea." He flicks through the pile of photos. "These are great. Well done." He stares at his beam-me-up-Scotty photo again and smiles. "OK, Jack, I'll see you later in class."

I don't show him the photos of inside the scrum. Not sure what I should do.

Chapter 9

Wee Puddles

Mum's sorting out books and I'm on a major job. She keeps coming over to check how it's going. "Looks good, Jack." I've spent all afternoon measuring and cutting a bigger hole for the flap in the back door. Ollie has no trouble getting through it, but Puppy is hopeless. Those wee puddles and poop accidents in the kitchen are happening all the time. Samantha's tired of cleaning them up. The other day, Nanna tripped and slid across the floor. A near puddle disaster.

My drill and tools are laid out in order on the porch. Samantha and Nanna watch me. Ollie's watching too, but Puppy's yapping. "Hey, quiet. And keep Puppy away. Just stay back."

Samantha picks up Puppy and rewards him with extra pats and cuddles. I roll my eyes at her. "Great training. Not."

Samantha doesn't care and keeps hugging Puppy. I think even Ollie rolls his eyes. I widen the opening. Check, adjust, file. Then I install the bigger doggy door. I flip it in and out. A few more adjustments. It's pretty good.

Mum calls out to me as she mixes the vegetable stir-fry. "That's wonderful, Jack. Puppy's going to love it."

"As long as he uses it. No more puddles inside."

"Can he try it?" Mum waves her wooden spoon in the air like a conductor. She's always got music inside her head. Maybe that's why my embarrassing mother dances around and does jumping jacks.

"Yep. All good to go."

"Come on, Puppy. You have to use this." Samantha pushes Puppy through the flap again and again. Suddenly Puppy gets it and jumps through the flap himself. Nanna claps. Mum does a jumping jack just as Rob comes bounding in with his new super dishwashing gloves. "Is that jumping jack for me?" He flashes the gloves around. "New product. Just came in at work."

I groan.

Rob notices the improved dog door. Stops. Checks it out. "Pretty good, Jack."

"Dinner's ready in a minute," Mum sings out. That means action. Dinner's family time, no excuses. There're scuffles as we scramble for the table. Samantha pulls out her chair, and gurgles, "You did such a great job, Jack. On the Puppy door."

Nanna beams. "Jack's a fixer. Can fix anything."

"That's why I'm here."

Mum's dishing out food.

I gulp down a whole carrot in one bite. "Great dinner, Mum."

Mum shines. She loves a compliment. We're eating, talking about the new door flap, when she casually says, "Oh, by the way, Leo's coming down this weekend. He hasn't seen Puppy yet. Or the Puppy door. And we want to see Leo." She glances at Rob. "He's part of our family."

Samantha nods. Nanna raises her eyebrows at me. She knows. Leo. What am I supposed to feel? He's not my brother. He's not like Sammy. He's OK. Mum looks at me. She brushes back her hair. Rob looks at me. He misses Leo. They want me to like him.

"Leo. That's great."

Rob bounces up from the table. "We can all surf." He's so excited. I don't feel excited. He heads for the sink and turns the faucet on to boiling. "Dishes, everyone."

I carry over plates. Steam is pumping out of the sink. "You'll get third-degree burns, Rob."

"Not with these new super-protective dishwashing gloves." He waves his yellow rubber hands in the air.

I laugh. I suppose I don't mind Leo really. He's a good surfer. Just that he's not my best mate and Rob goes strange when he stays. It's like no one else exists when Leo arrives. It's fine, I guess. It's not like Rob is my real dad.

I pin a new photo of Anna with the red ribbons in her hair on my photo wall. She gave me one of the ribbons. It smells like roses. Like her.

Grandad's photo is right next to it. I stare at the photo. I hear Grandad's voice. "Jack, you've got to find the answers you need." I don't know how, Grandad. Tell me how. The face in the small photo at the bottom of my wall glares at me. It's my father, wherever he is, whoever he is.

I look out into the hallway and see a light coming from Nanna's room. I knock on her door. "Come in." Nanna looks up from her armchair where it sits overlooking the garden. She puts down her book — *Advanced Bridge Rules*.

"Bridge?"

"I'll have to teach you one day." Nanna smiles.

"One day." I pick up one of her bridge trophies from her side table. "You're so smart, Nanna." There's a small tapestry in a gold frame on the wall just above the side table. *Nil desperandum*. There's a translation underneath. *Never despair.* I look at Nanna.

"Your Grandad always believed there was a way forward. Not to give up and despair." Nanna looks at it. "Grandad really liked the tapestry. I can't embroider these days with my arthritis." She rubs her hands.

There's a photo of Grandad in Vietnam in his khaki uniform next to the tapestry. "Grandad always said that you have to defend what you believe in. War is the last resort. He didn't like war."

Nanna gets up and walks towards the tapestry. "You're so much like your grandad. A hero."

"I'm not, Nanna."

Nanna stares at the photo. "When your father left, Grandad was here. I loved watching you work with him. Fixing things together."

"Wish he was here, Nanna."

"I do too." Nanna presses her hand against the tapestry. "His heart attack was so sudden. And you were just a boy running for Mum and me."

I feel my legs running. Grandad lying on the ground and calling for help. I whisper, "I didn't save him, Nanna. I should have saved him."

Nanna gasps. "Don't ever say that. Ever. You were the last person he saw. That was a gift to him, Jack. He loved you so much." She puts her hand over mine. "We pulled together afterward. Just like he'd want. Your mum was strong, but you were strong too. And you got stronger. It takes all kinds to be heroes."

I go back to my room.

"Hector, do you want some cookie crumbs?"

His white tail flicks as I dribble crumbs into his cage. Thinking. Thinking. I go to my computer and type the words carefully. I print out *Nil desperandum*. *Never despair*. I pin it on my photo wall next to Grandad.

Chapter 10

Cliff Tops and Beaches

The wind bites into my face this morning as I pedal down the streets. I fling my last newspaper into the last house on the street and it skids to the front door. A man in pajamas comes out. "Good throw."

I wave and start to bike home. A couple of dogs chase me down the street and I pedal harder. They give up. Suddenly I don't want to go home. I swerve into a side street, skimming over rocks on the dirt track. Birds whistle as I jump broken branches and race to the cliff tops.

Puffing, I skid my bike to a stop and stare out to sea. The waves crash against the rocks. The beach is quiet. Grandad used to take me down there. I leave my bike at the cliff top and climb down the track. It's steep and the loose dirt and rocks roll under my feet. I grab on to trees so I don't slide to the bottom.

The sun's up but the beach still looks gray. I sit on the sand and stare out at the waves, thinking. I shiver. I don't know how it happens, but Grandad is next to me. He's wearing his blue-flannel checked shirt and khaki work pants, holding the ring wrench. The twelve-point one. "You're going to be thirteen soon. It's a big birthday. What do you want?"

It's hard to breathe. "I want you to be here, Grandad."

"I'm here. We're a team. I'm always here for you, Jack."

I nod my head. "And Dad's gone too. I've asked Mum. She won't talk about him. Why'd he go?"

Grandad doesn't say anything for a long time. I feel his arm on my shoulder. "The answers are there. But you have to decide when you want to find them."

We sit there watching the waves crash and roll onto the sand.

I wander into the kitchen and pick up an apple.

Mum points to the clock. "You're late. Did you deliver more newspapers this morning?"

"Yeah, Mum."

"I've got breakfast for you. And can we talk about your birthday party? We can have it on your actual birthday. But you need to send out the invitations soon."

"Can we talk about it later?"

Mum's voice follows me down the hallway. "Are you all right?"

"Great, Mum. Great." I shut my bedroom door, get on to my computer. I bring up my to-do ideas list:

1. *Birthday*
2. *Soundboard*
3. *Photos of game for newsletter*
4. *Rugby game film clip*
5. *Surf*
6. *Leo staying*
7. *Ethics homework*
8. *Grandad*

I draw a line through number three since I've given the photos to Mr. Angelou already. I add:

9. *Father*

A joke flashes into my head. "Why is six afraid of seven?" Then I laugh. "Because seven eight nine." "Eight, ate … nine." I can't stop laughing, laughing, until I'm rolling on the floor. Until I'm lying on the floor. Until I don't move. Until I just lie there thinking. I pull myself up, check out my photo wall. Look at Grandad, then the picture in the bottom corner. I go back to my computer and type the question: *How do I find my father?*

Rob's acting strange again because Leo's coming down for the weekend. He polished his van for hours. You need blinkers to get near it. He bought a surfboard for Leo ages ago and waxed it until now it has perfect grip. It's in the shed right next to my very old board. I really need to give it a wax.

There's a pile of new T-shirts and board shorts for Leo on the fold-up bed in my room. Rob did buy me one T-shirt. I admit that I like it. Scrawled across it is Albert Einstein's theory of relativity: $E=mc^2$ — *Albert Einstein*. He's my science hero. Rob bought Mum and

Samantha matching rainbow scarves. They both love them.

Toot. Toot. The yellow van rocks into the driveway and Mum dances to the front door. She's so much better now. Her surgery doesn't hurt her anymore. "They're here," she sings.

Ollie's woofing. Nanna waddles out. Samantha races down the hallway. Puppy tumbles after her through the super dog-flap door. Puss is on the window ledge looking out. Rob stands beside the van with his hand on Leo's shoulder. I get this lump in my throat.

"Leo's here. So, is dinner ready?" Rob whistles.

Mum's smile crumples. "But I worked today and I thought you'd —"

Rob laughs and produces a huge tub of roast chicken from the van. "Here's dinner, babe."

Leo holds up an enormous bag of hot potato wedges.

"Oh! And *I've* made the salads," Mum pipes up.

Nanna grins. "I've got dessert. Cream buns for everyone."

Dinner's a feast, but quick. Tonight is movie night. Boys' pick, but girls welcome. Seven o'clock on the dot, there's a *knock-knock* on the door. It's Mr. Napoli dropping off Anna. She's carrying a supersized bowl of berries of all sorts. It's an Italian thing. You can't visit unless you bring food. A lot of it. Since I love berries, it's working out pretty well.

"Hello, Jack," Mr. Napoli bellows through the front door. Wow, is he red-faced and excited.

Anna slips inside with the berries. Rob waves from the kitchen sink. He's on serious dishwashing duty. Mr. Napoli calls out, "Hello, Rob." Rob waves but can't leave the sink.

Mr. Napoli hardly takes time to kiss Mum on both cheeks before he gets into it. "Anna. Anna. She's made us very proud. The school picked her slogan for their charity project with Room to Read. It'll be in the newsletters and on all the posters."

"Jack told me." Mum's nearly as excited as Mr. Napoli.

Anna isn't excited. "Dad." She's at the door again, seriously giving dagger looks. "Please, no more showing off, Dad."

"A father needs to show off. Anna's slogan is: 'Every Kid Deserves to Read.' They interviewed her on the radio."

"I heard it." Mum beams. "She was wonderful."

"Yes. She is wonderful. I am so —"

"Dad. Go now. Go."

"A father can be proud." He double kisses Anna as she shoves him towards his car.

Anna shakes her head. "He's so embarrassing."

"Hey, don't worry. He's your dad."

Anna's lucky. I like Mr. Napoli. I grab her hand and pull her into the family room. "Movie night."

She plonks herself down between Samantha and Puppy. Ollie's at their feet. The berries are on the coffee table. Nanna's popping corn. "Nearly ready," she shouts.

"Drinks. What do you want?" Mum's got a new juicer. "Celery juice, or beet and carrot juice, or watermelon juice? Choose your poison."

Mum's right about the poison. We all call out, "Watermelon."

"Down with celery juice," I yell.

"Don't yell, Jack. And celery juice is good for you."

"Reeeeeeeally good, if you're a rabbit."

Mum's getting flustered, but when we all burst out laughing, she can't help laughing as well. "Maybe watermelon for me too, this time."

"Stop messing around," Rob calls out. "Movie time."

I drag two beanbags in front of the TV. Leo dives into one and I dive into the other.

"Come on, babe. Sit down. We're ready." Rob holds up *The Endless Summer*. He becomes serious and the lecture starts. "Before we watch this classic, you need some background information. Chasing the waves around the world. Sun, surf, freedom. Following Californian longboarders Mike Hynson and Robert August —"

"Put it on, Rob. Let's see it."

"But, Jack, this is a film classic …" Rob scratches his prickly head and continues.

I can't take it. I grab a cushion and aim. Rob ducks as it torpedoes towards him. He yells. "JACK!"

"It wasn't me." Rob turns around and there's Mum giggling with a second cushion.

"You! But —" The cushion flies towards Rob. He ducks.

We're all laughing, Leo pipes up. "Let's see the movie, Dad."

"Yeah, Dad. Let's see it." Oh, I can't believe it. I didn't mean to call Rob "Dad." Why did I do that? Hope no one noticed. Think fast. I chuck another cushion at Rob. Leo copies. Anna does a lollipop throw then winks at me. I can't believe it. She knows. *She knows about the cricket match.* Cushions are flying, dogs are woofing and Puss is looking on as if to say, Are they nuts?

"I give up. Give up." Rob's smothered in cushions. You can only see his hands flapping. "I'm getting up. Just hold on." He presses play. *The Endless Summer* rolls on the screen with endless waves, endless tubes, the endless summer.

"I ate too much popcorn." Leo holds his stomach, groaning as he checks out my photo wall. I made sure a couple of photos of him with Rob are pinned up. There're plenty of other photos of Rob too — blowing up the barbecue, Rob and Mum when she was in the hospital, Rob in the van with me. "You do a lot with my dad. I don't get to see him that much." Leo gets into the fold-up bed and stares at my photo wall. "Great pictures."

I get this sad feeling for Leo. I like my home. Rob's not my dad, but he's here. I stammer, "Maybe you can visit some more. My birthday's soon. Want to come to my party?"

Leo waits. Nods. "Yeah, that'd be good."

I get into my bed. "Surfing tomorrow."

"Like surfing." Leo looks at me with a challenge. "With my dad."

"Rob likes surfing." I press my lips together. "With you. He talks about you a lot." I wait. "Your dad misses you, Leo."

Leo gulps. "Yeah. Me too."

I switch off the bedside light and look out of the window. The night's calm. The moon's getting bigger. Leo's breathing is deep and regular. I listen to him. I'm going to find my dad. I shut my eyes.

Chapter 11

Bags Can Fly

Had a great day surfing. Heaps of guys and girls out there. Took a crazy video of Rob getting hammered by a monster wave. He came out spluttering but trying to be cool. "Just testing out the wave. It won that time. Ha-ha." I had some wipeouts myself. It was a big surf today.

Anna and Maggie turned up with drinks and sandwiches. I didn't even know they were coming to the beach — and we were thirsty and starving. Rob said they're angels. Anna smiled, shaking her head. "I don't think so." But she is, you know. An angel. Got some great shots of the girls and one of Leo looking dopey at Maggie. I reckon he likes Maggie.

Sunday night. I can tell Leo doesn't want to go back north. He's so slow packing up and keeps looking at my photo wall. "Hey, I'll send you photos." I grin. "There's some good ones of Maggie."

Leo prickles. "What do ya mean?"

"Nothing. But I'll send you some of Maggie anyway."

Rob shouts, "Leo, we've got to go. The train won't wait."

Leo grabs his backpack and heads for the car with Rob. Team family — Mum, Nanna, Samantha, Ollie and Puppy and even Puss — pile onto the porch to say good-bye. Leo sticks his head out of the window and waves.

I call out, "See you for my birthday party."

Mum puts her arm through mine. "It means a lot to me that you boys get on. To Rob too. So Leo's coming to your party?"

My head thumps. I'm glad Mum's happy, but I don't want her to say anything. I don't know what I feel.

It's late. Everyone's asleep except me: I can't. My mind is all over the place. I keep thinking about Rob. Why'd I call him Dad? I need to find my dad. Hey, Anna knew I dropped the ball for her at the game. She wasn't even angry and she could have been. She really stands up for fair play. Suddenly the *scrum* zigzags into my head. Fair play. That wasn't fair. What am I supposed to do? I sit up in my bed. I am so awake. The game. I can't sleep. Might as well do some editing.

I grab my laptop, soundboard and flash drive, creak open my bedroom door and pad down the hallway, through the back door onto the porch. The dog flap swings and bangs. I lurch down to stop it. Don't want to wake up Ollie and Puppy. That'd be a disaster. I run across the driveway to the shed and knock into Rob's punching bag. It nearly takes me out. Phew: somehow I get inside the shed without waking anyone up. I switch on the light. The place is looking pretty good after the cleanup. I put my soundboard on my bench, plug in my laptop and set up.

I turn on my computer. There's a lot of footage and a lot of editing to do. But I've got to think what I want to do with it. Anyway, speakers first. I like the night, when it's quiet. When everyone's asleep and it's just me working. I'm listening to some of the sound tracks when I nearly hit the roof.

Mum's voice comes out of nowhere. "It's late. Why are you here? What are you doing, Jack?"

I look up at Mum. "Mu-ummmmmm ... what are you wearing? That snapdragon. Is it blood-sucking?"

"Ha-ha." Mum flips the end of her nightie around her legs. The orange snapdragon looks like it's eating her knees. "Don't you like my new nightie, darling?"

"No, Mum, and don't call me darling."

She laughs and looks over my shoulder. I shut down the screen just as Coach's voice comes on — "George: now. Now! Kill 'em. Kill 'em."

"What's that?"

"Nothing. It's just an assignment. Just want to get a head start. I'm doing some work on it with Christopher tomorrow after school before Strategy Day."

"Tomorrow's the start of a new week. You'll be tired for your paper route."

"Won't be long. Hey, you go to bed, Mum." She looks unsure. "I'll be in soon."

"Promise?"

"Yeah, yeah. Soon."

"Love you, Jack."

"Same to you." I wait until Mum leaves, and check that she doesn't pop back in. She's gone. It's safe to get to work again. I look at the footage. Stop, rewind. Play. I don't know what to put in. Should I put everything in? That's the game. Hawkie's nose was smashed. No one tells. Hawkie's too scared. He'd lose his mates. Maybe worse. Christopher didn't see inside the scrum. I guess I should show him all the footage. See what he thinks.

Monday morning. Mrs. Napoli calls. Rob answers, puts her on speaker so we can all hear. "The electricity went out on some of our fridges. Anna has to help empty the goods. She'll be late and we can't give her a ride. We need to clean up and wait for the electricity company. Can you take Anna to school?"

"No worries," Rob says. "Might as well give everyone a ride."

I get in the backseat as usual. Anna jumps in next to me. "The fridges are leaking everywhere."

"Is the shop OK now?"

"Under control." She clicks in her seat belt. "Hey, Jack, heard you're having a birthday party?"

"Who told you, Anna?" I tap Samantha on the shoulder.

The guilty party looks around. "I told." She flicks her ponytail at me.

"Am I invited?" Anna's voice tinkles.

"No, never." I try to keep a serious face.

"So what time, date and what kind of party is it?"

"Three weeks on Saturday. My backyard. Six o'clock." Pretending to be on a wave, I hold out my arms. "A surfing party. Hawaiian shirts, pineapples, *The Endless Summer* on a video loop. It'll be endless."

Rob interrupts. "This is all the result of having a great stepdad." He laughs. "Jack, we could wear matching Hawaiian shirts. Red hibiscus."

"Great idea, Rob. It'd really improve my image.

We'd be the original Hawaiian Nerd Squad."

Anna ignores us. It's all about the party. "Want some help?"

"Yes, please. A lot of it."

"I'll help too," Samantha pipes up.

"Great. So, this Saturday, I'll be over and we can get the invitations done. So much to do."

"Huh?" Anna's so organized. What is there to do? Rob's laughing. I hit the back of his seat. "OK, it's a plan."

Rob drops us off. Kids point and yell out at his van. He loves it and toots his horn. He's becoming the coolest stepdad at school. Samantha runs off to her friends. Anna runs over to Maggie. I can hear her. She's talking about my birthday. I roll my eyes. Got to find Christopher. Need to ask him about the film. Where is he? I spot him coming out of the bathroom. Then he starts prowling under benches. I shout out and growl. "Found a tiger yet?"

Christopher doesn't even hear me. I race up and nudge him. "What're you doing?"

His face is panicky. "My bag's gone."

"Where'd you leave it?"

"Just outside. Here. A minute ago."

"Maybe someone's picked it up by accident? They all look the same."

"Yeah, but mine has my name on it and a Navy tag."

"Navy as in ships? Or blue?"

"Ships," Christopher grunts as he crawls under another bench.

"Why do you have a Navy tag?"

"Jack … What does it matter? I got it when the Navy ships were in. I need to find my bag."

Oh, I didn't know Christopher liked the Navy. I'd like to have a look inside a ship. "Christopher?"

"Yeeeesssss." Christopher's voice is shaky.

I think I'll ask him later about the Navy ships. I scout around the outside of the hall. But no bag. "Let's see if it's been handed in at the office."

Christopher keeps looking at everyone's bags as we cross the playground. Winger's spinning a ball to Hawkie, who's gasping for air under his bandages. I figure he doesn't want to play. He should stand up for himself. Guess it's easier to say than do. Winger sees us and starts laughing. Don't know what's so funny.

We go inside to the school office.

"No one's reported a missing bag." The secretary takes a note. "If it's handed in I'll get it announced." She turns away to talk to a parent.

"But it's got my homework in it." Christopher sounds desperate, but the secretary isn't listening.

"Hey, it'll show up, Christopher. Don't worry."

Everyone's already in their seats when we get to

class. Mr. Angelou's annoyed. "Why are you boys late?" He doesn't wait for an answer. "We've got a lot of work to do. Get your homework out."

I scramble through my bag, push aside my camera and drag out my homework. Lucky I've done it. Shoving it towards Christopher, I nudge him. "Let's share. My turn for a change." He's tapping the desk nervously. "Hey, we'll find your bag. It's got to be around."

I hear Winger smirking. George Hamel and Hawkie are nudging each other and staring out the window behind Mr. Angelou. Becky splutters. "Flying bag." I look through the window. Christopher sees it too and gulps. The Navy tag. His bag is swinging at half-mast from the flagpole. There're laughs coming from the back. Mr. Angelou spins, glares around the class. He's furious. "Quiet. Do your work *now*."

Winger looks like he's nearly exploding trying to control belly laughs. I elbow Christopher. "Come on, let's tell Mr. Angelou."

"No. We don't know who did it. I don't want any trouble." Christopher's voice is breathless.

"It's got to be Winger. I'm not scared."

"I'm not either." But I can see he is. Christopher adjusts his glasses. "Got to be sure."

Mr. Angelou's voice booms across the room. "When I say quiet, I mean it."

The class settles down. Christopher keeps looking up at his bag swinging in the wind. At the bell, he shoves me out of my seat.

"Hey, I'm movin', I'm movin'." I grab my camera, and we race to the flagpole. It's there, hanging, with the Navy tag flapping. *Click. Click. Click.* Photographic evidence. Never know when you'll need it. I pull the rope and the bag jerks down.

Christopher grabs it, checks that everything's safe inside it. One of the straps is torn off. "Oh no. It's new. Mum just bought it and it cost a lot. They can't afford to … I *have* to fix it."

"It's all right. I've got a staple gun in the shed. I fix lots of stuff like this." Christopher's face is dotted with sweat. "Why don't we just talk to Mr. Angelou? I've got the photos."

"Leave it, Jack. OK?"

I shake my head. I don't like this, but Christopher's pulling my sleeve. "OK."

Chapter 12

Ping. Ping.

Samantha's puffing. "Jack, Anna, Christopher … my project … my …"

"Hey, breathe, Sammy. What's up?"

"It won best project. It's in the library with a blue first-place ribbon on it. Come and see."

I don't want to go, but Samantha's desperate. "Got to be quick. Can't miss the bus."

We run into the library past Mrs. Lopez, who calls out. "Don't run in the library." Then she smiles. "Great project, Samantha."

There it is. In the middle of the room. Got to admit, the dog-elephant looks great since its nose operation. "Fantastic!" Anna hugs Samantha.

Christopher nods, but doesn't say anything.

"Good one, Sammy." I take some quick photos.

We pile onto the school bus. Samantha can't stop talking about her award-winning dog project. Anna listens and says, "It's wonderful, Sammy."

We pile off the school bus. The Tran Bakery sign is just ahead. "Better get home, Sammy, and tell Nanna and Mum the dog news." I smile at Anna. "Christopher and I've got to do an assignment for school." I pretend to punch Samantha on her arm. "You're a winner, Sammy." Her face lights up.

Christopher and I walk inside the bakery. Mr. Tran is behind the counter. "Hi, Mr. Tran."

"Hello, boys. Good day at school?"

"Sure, Dad." Christopher slings the bag over his shoulder with the good strap. He grabs some cheese rolls from the shelves.

It's great having a friend who lives in a bakery. Mrs. Tran gives us a bottle of orange juice each from the drinks fridge. "Your nanna was in today."

"Nanna loves your cookies."

Mrs. Tran's eyes crinkle into a smile. "I know."

Christopher's room is on top of the shop. We sit on his bed. "Can we swap bags? They look the same, except for the Navy tag. I've got an Einstein tag."

"Why do that?"

"I'll repair your bag tonight. I'm good with a staple

gun. We can swap again tomorrow. No one will know. What do you think?" He takes off his glasses, rubs his forehead with his hands. "What do ya think?" I ask him again.

After what seems ages, he nods. "Thanks, Jack."

We empty our bags, swap them and repack. Then we eat the cheese rolls and drink the orange juice. After that, we're ready. We sit at Christopher's desk, open up my laptop and get on to the video of the rugby game. The screen lights up with shots of George Hamel running. He has great moves. He's a natural. I won't ever be that good a rugby player. Winger's really fast. There's lots of action shots between the Reds and Blues.

"It's good, Jack." Christopher's in a better mood now.

The crowd scenes are funny. Anna's jumping with her hair spreading out, glinting in the sun. Christopher nudges me. "A lot of coverage of Anna."

"Yeah." As quick as I can, I flick to other sequences. "Hey, look at this." Becky's mouth is open so wide you can see her tonsils. She's screaming, "George Hamel!" We laugh so hard we're rolling over each other and I fall off my chair.

Christopher's the first to stop. "Hey, let's get … ha-ha-ha-ha-ha … on with … this … ha-ha-ha."

Holding on to my sides, I stop laughing and sit back onto my chair.

"Let's work with the Becky clips. You've done a great job with the soundboard so we can do something good." Christopher gets up the edit tools and we work on editing, changes, reediting. Time disappears. Looks right. We nod at each other and slap hands. "Let's see what we've got, Jack." Christopher presses play. Becky's scream repeats, repeats, "George, George, George!" as Becky and Jasmin jump in the air. It's good. Really good.

I can see Christopher feels better. Maybe I can tell him about the scrum now?

"Hey, Christopher," I stammer. "Can I show …"

Christopher glances at his phone. "It's getting late. Mr. Angelou reserved the computer lab room for us for Strategy Day. Let's do the rest then."

"But I want to —"

Ping. Ping. Christopher glances at his phone again. I look down at mine.

Facebook messages:

Legend: Hey, 4 eyes. Chink a chonk. Find your bag?

A badly Photoshopped photo comes up of a pig wearing Christopher's black-framed glasses.

Hotchic2: Oink, oink!

There're nearly twenty "oinks" after it.

Likes: 25. Shares: 2.

I hold up my phone. "What's goin' on?"

"Nothing."

"It's that idiot, Winger, and his stupid girlfriend, Jasmin, isn't it? They need something between their ears, other than air. I bet George Hamel's in on this too."

Christopher adjusts his glasses. It's becoming a nervous habit. "Can't have any trouble."

"You won't, Christopher. Just let's sort it out. I've got photos of your bag on the flagpole!"

"Mum and Dad. They don't need this. Not with working so hard in the bakery. Just leave it alone, Jack. It'll sort out."

This sick feeling grips my stomach. Stuff like this doesn't sort out. Christopher adjusts his glasses again. "If you're my mate, you'll let me handle it."

"I am your mate." We sit silently. Christopher doesn't look at me.

Mrs. Tran's voice makes us both jump. She opens the door. "Have you finished your work?"

"Yes, Mum." Christopher gets up.

He waves through the shop window at me as I head off. I turn around and see him behind the counter helping his parents stack bread on the shelves.

Ollie sees me coming. He runs to the front gate, wagging his tail.

"Hi, mate. Did ya have a good day with Puppy?" I look up at the house. Mum's singing and Samantha's yapping. I can hear Puppy yapping with her. She's got to be still telling Mum all about her dog-elephant project. I don't feel like going into the house. Ollie follows me down the driveway. I drop Christopher's bag at the front of the shed and give a slug to Rob's punching bag. It comes back and I slug it again. I start jabbing it, left-right-left-right, then belt into it. Squinting my eyes, the bag blurs, everything blurs as my brain goes into outer space like a *Star Trek* voyage through asteroids:

Christopher's trying to tell, but Becky and Jasmin

are giggling hilariously. No one can hear him. His bag's swinging on the flagpole that spearheads into a scrum. Winger and George are panting down the field into Hawkie whose nose is bleeding and bleeding. Anna's amazing smile gets wider and wider until it turns into a pig wearing Christopher's glasses. Dad's pointing at Rob, then me, with Grandad's voice buzzing in my head. Nil desperandum. *Never despair. You can find the answers.*

Suddenly Ollie's pulling at my socks and is woofing, woofing. Breathless, I stop hitting the punching bag, lean against the shed, pat Ollie, who licks my hand. I pick up Christopher's bag, and open the shed door. Ollie follows me inside to the workbench. I empty the backpack. Get out my staple gun and position it so the staples aren't near where Christopher's shoulder will go. It feels good working on the bag strap, fixing something. I take my hammer down from my pegboard, knock the staples hard into place. That strap won't break now. I hold out the bag.

"Come on, Ollie. Outside." It's starting to get dark. The moon's out already. It's nearly a half-moon tonight. The smell of baking wafts from the kitchen into the garden. Mum's making banana cakes for the Room to Read treat stall. I bend down and hold Ollie's face. "Kitchen, Ollie. Go to Mum. Treats." His tail goes into super-drive. He pushes through the flap door and heads for Mum.

"Oh, Ollie, where did you come from?" *Woof, woof.*
"Do you want a treat?" *Woof. Woof.* I sneak past Mum
and into my room.

"Hi, Hector." I crumble a few cookie crumbs into
his cage, then sit at my desk. I turn on my computer.
Search. Obituaries come up. There're thousands
of them. "Boat Harbour. Date." Grandad's funeral
notice flashes up. I click to open it. Read, then reread,
then reread. *Beloved grandfather of Jack and Samantha.*
Deeply missed. I rub my eyes. I'm not going to cry.

I'm going to fix things. Find answers.

Chapter 13

Strategy Day

EVERY KID DESERVES TO READ

Room to Read has helped over 9 million children to access books and education.

ROOMTOREAD.ORG

Room to Read®

Poster design by Anna Napoli

The school's plastered with Anna's posters. Anna's amazing. Samantha and I carry Mum's banana cakes to the hall for the Room to Read treat stall. The tables already have plenty of cheese-stick swirls, tubs of popcorn, pineapple-and-melon kebabs, berry baskets and cupcakes. Mr. Angelou made a strawberry cheesecake. There are two cupcakes with glowing green icing. They look pretty good. I rattle my pocket. Worth getting up early to do the newspaper route. I've got plenty of money.

"Hey, Anna. Banana cakes for your stall."

"That's fantastic. Put them over there."

"Can I buy some cupcakes? The two green ones and …" I nudge Samantha. "Which one do you want, Sammy?"

"Pink."

"What a surprise."

"I'm not supposed to sell them before the stall opens." Anna flicks a curl. "But you brought in two banana cakes. Yep, it's fair that you get to go first."

I hand her some money. "Your posters are great, Anna. Really great."

The bell rings. Mr. Angelou's voice comes over the PA. "Attention Strategy-Day classes, go to your groups now. To remind you:

Mrs. Banneker — Discovering herbs is in the eco garden."

My view: Science nerds welcome. Like *me*.

"Coach — Training for fitness in the gym."

My view: Coach needs to train to be human. Grrr.

"Photo editing — Jack and Christopher in the computer lab."

My view: Important.

"Mr. Angelou — my group — Books That Changed the World in the library."

My view: One guess which book will star? It's got a *bird* in the title.

"There's a treat stall at morning break. All proceeds go to Room to Read. Now everyone move quickly and quietly to your areas and enjoy the day."

Kids are going in all directions. Christopher and I are going against the crowd, but eventually make it to the computer lab. Lots of computers, parts, plugs. Feels like home. We set up the laptop, sound, editing and everything else we need. "Ready?" I press play and the photos we've edited with the sound track run like a film clip on the screen. It's fast and action-packed.

"It's really good, Jack."

"Yep. But I have something else I want to show you. No one else has seen it." He stops. "You won't like it."

"Why? What's in it?"

"You'll see." I press play again. The Reds and Blues

huddle in a pack, crouching down, the front rows interlock hands and heads. The voice-over of the ref calls out. The ball's thrown in and it's like a mass of wasps. The hookers kick into the scrum with cleats and spikes; mud and grass splatter. There are fast close-ups of a Red hand yanking a Blue's ear. Blurs of George Hamel's face with a killer look. His fingers dig into a Blue player's leg. Reds smash ankles. The sounds of cracking, grunting, screams. Then it's all Winger. He drives his arm back, his elbow belting into Hawkie's face. Hawkie's groaning, blood … A lot of blood.

I stop. Replay. Stop. Replay. Hawkie's face takes up the whole screen.

Christopher takes off his glasses. Rubs the lenses, then looks at me. He stammers, "What do you want to do, Jack?"

"Make the video." Christopher looks unsure. "We've got to."

Once we start Christopher just wants to do the best job. "Do you reckon we should take that angle? Slide in Coach's 'Kill 'em'?"

"Maybe edge Winger in over the top of Hawkie?"

We cut, edit. End up with Mr. Angelou up George Hamel's nose. It's crazy and funny and so good working together. The time goes fast and we don't think about what it all means.

When Mr. Angelou sticks his head into the computer lab and calls out, "How's it going?" we nearly jump out of our skins. "Gave you a shock, eh? Sorry." But he's smirking, so he's not that sorry. "Can I have a quick look at what you've done?"

A thud pounds inside my chest. Christopher closes his eyes in a squint. I stumble over my words. "It's not ready yet, sir. Can we show you when it is?"

"Of course." We just look at Mr. Angelou until he gets the message. "OK. I'd better go check the other groups and get back to mine before they realize I've gone." He leaves.

"Jack, maybe you shouldn't give it to Mr. Angelou? He'll show the school. What'll Winger do when he finds out you made it? George Hamel? Coach? They'll kill us. We won't ever be able to go to games again. Even the girls will hate us. Maybe it's not a good idea."

"Your name won't be on it, Christopher."

"But they'll know I've worked on it with you."

"I won't do anything without talking to you, Christopher. We just have to think about it."

Christopher isn't sure. "I guess."

We eat our green cupcakes. "Not as good as the cakes from the Tran Bakery." Christopher smiles. I nearly fall off my seat. I smile back at him. He nearly falls off his seat. We stand up, peer into the mirror above the computer. We both lift our lips with our index fingers. Stare into the mirror, then at each other. Then into the mirror. Yes, we've definitely turned Martian. We can't stop laughing. Our teeth are fluorescent, radiating slime green.

Anna can't remember who donated the cupcakes to the treat stall and no one's owning up. Going home on the bus is crazy. We flash our teeth at everyone. Becky nearly hits the roof when I flash them at her with a special-effects Dracula drool. It's so much fun.

Paul's asked me before about the paper route. He wants to make some pocket money. I need some time. The newspaper man knows Paul and he's had a trial run with me. The newspaper man won't care, as long as the papers are delivered. There's so much in my head and I'm on the computer every night now until really late.

Jack: Can ya do the papers tomorrow? Paid work. What about sharing the route?

Ping. Ping. Check my messages. Talk about quick.

Paul: Great. Sure thing.

I call the newspaper man, then message Paul back. I brush my teeth for ages. The green's fading. I pull out my chair, take out my laptop, open the screen. Press *Search.* I search for my father. I've searched every nearby town. I've searched hospitals. I've searched his name with every spelling I can think of ... I search. A notice flashes up. Just a line. Not again. This notice comes up all the time in my searches.

My dates and the hospital and Mum and Dad's names. The heading: *Jack was born.*

I already knew I was born.

Chapter 14

Crazy Saturday

It's here. Crazy Saturday. Birthday invitations. Girls are everywhere in the kitchen. Mum's bought cardboard, ribbons, sparkles, colored pencils, paste. Nanna's in charge of sparkles. She has them set up in a row like medicine bottles. Samantha's arranging tubs of sand, shells and seaweed on the table. Anna's arrived with tiny plastic surfboards. They scream. Mum does jumping jacks in her new flouncy cinnamon-swirl dress. Puppy's in a tug-of-war, mangling Mum's strappy sandals. Rob barges in, then barges out, shouting. "Need to mow the lawn."

"I'll help," I call after him.

"No you won't." Mum does a cinnamon leap nearly onto my toe.

"Hey, watch out, Mum. Your dress is blinding me. Let me get my sunglasses."

"Ha, no escape, Jack." Mum's face creases. "We need to know how you'd like your invitations to look. Then who you're inviting."

"Mum, I can just message everyone."

"That's not a proper invitation to a thirteenth birthday. This is an important one." I look around. Four pairs of eyes glue me down, like a bug in a spider's web. I can see that I'm not going to get out of this.

"OK." I sink into a chair at the table.

"So what sort of invitation cards do you want, Jack?"

"Anything."

Mum ignores my comment. "Well, it's a surfing theme."

Anna holds up the miniature surfboards.

"Where'd you buy them?" Nanna's teeth flip out, but she's quick and in no time they're back in.

"I found them at Susie's Super Discount Store."

"A bargain?" Nanna gets excited at the thought of any bargain.

"Yes." Anna twirls her curls. There're cheers from every direction. I groan. This is going to be a loooooong afternoon.

Cutting, pasting, sticking, drawing. Disasters, like the wrong colored ribbon, and major breakdowns because, for example, the surfboards won't stick. I'm going to die here. "Jack, what do you think of this?" Mum asks, holding up my name. "JACK."

"Great."

"Jack, what do you think of this?" Anna asks. It's a blue ribbon.

"Great."

"Jack, what do you think of this?" Samantha asks. It's a green ribbon.

"Great." I think my brain has melted. My eyes are glazed. Rob's still mowing the lawn. It's the longest mow ever. Why has he left me stranded? I want to mow too. Oh no, Nanna's turn.

"Jack, do you need a drink. Juice?"

Sigh. I love Nanna. "Yessssss. I'll make some for everyone. Just need to squeeze some oranges." It's my smart plan. I'll take ages and ages to do it. The juice is a bonus.

I'm at the fridge, slowly getting out oranges. Slowly cutting them. Slowly squeezing them in the juicer. Slowly getting glasses. Slowly pouring it out. I stand watching them. They're laughing and chatting about the invitations for my thirteenth birthday. The most important thing in the world. Suddenly, a warm feeling passes through me like sunlight. I pick up my camera. *Click. Click. Click.* Samantha notices and makes a face. *Click. Click. Click.* Nanna's laughing so hard she sneezes glitter all over her cookies. *Click. Click. Click.* Mum fluffs her hair.

I shout out the window. "Fresh orange juice." Rob waves. "Rob, the grass is screaming for help. If you don't stop, it's going to look like your head." *Click. Click. Click.* Screaming grass.

"Keep the juice for me. Nearly finished." Rob gives me a how-smart-am-I look.

"You know, the invitations are pretty much done, Rob."

"Oh, is that right?" Rob turns off the mower. "Then the lawn's done."

I roll my eyes. "Dead and buried, more like."

There's a major post-invitation cleanup going on. I'm in charge of the garbage removal. "Make sure you put that in the recycling bin, Jack."

"Mum, as if I wouldn't. You're talking to a scientist here."

It's done. Tidy, clean, ready. Anna has the pile of cards. "Jack, you sit on the couch." I do what I'm told on this crazy invitation day, especially by Anna. Samantha is Anna's assistant. Rob arrives. Everyone's here and ready.

We're all looking at Anna. "I know we've annoyed you, Jack."

"Nooo … Not true," I lie.

Everyone laughs. "Yeee-esss … True, true, true."

"OK, a bit true."

"But we want your birthday to be the best ever, because," Anna blushes, "you are the best."

I go red. Mum giggles and nudges Rob. I give her a glare. Mum stops giggling. Anna turns to Samantha, who hands her an invitation. Anna holds it up, displaying the front. It glitters and sparkles. There's a hole cut in it. You can see the miniature surfboard. Across the front is *School's Out* in flowing capitals.

Samantha opens it and hands it to Anna. Inside is a beach scene with sand, shells and seaweed. It reads:

Surf's In

Get Amped
For The Endless Summer
At Jack's thirteenth
You're invited to drop in and ride the wave

Anna and Samantha are jumping up and down.
"Do you like it? Do you? Do you?"

I like it.

I'm making a list of people to invite to my birthday.

Christopher, Paul, Leo, Anna, Maggie, Samantha, the whole soccer team. I can't leave anyone out. Should I invite the rugby team? Well, Paul's coming. I like some of the other guys but … I'll think about it tomorrow.

OK, back to what I do every night. Look for Dad. I press *Search*.

Chapter 15

The Eagle

My door creaks open. "Jack, you're late for your paper route."

"Go away, Mum. Paul's doing my paper route today." Groaning, I roll over. Mum closes the door. I was up super late last night. Thought I had a lead. Sleep. Sleep. More sleep.

"Jack, Jack, Jack. Breakfaaaaast," Samantha screeches down the hallway. I open my eyes. Look at the clock. 8:15 a.m. Close my eyes.

The door bangs open. "Breakfast, lazy. Get up. We'll be late for school."

I chuck a pillow at Samantha. "Go away." She doesn't.

Mum's hair fuzzes through the door. "What's wrong, Jack?"

Oh no, she's on my case. Groan. "Headache, Mum."

Rob arrives. "What's up?" I jam my other pillow over my head but I can tell they're all just standing there. Ugh.

Nanna waddles through the door. "Jack."

"Anyone else want to come in?" I sit up and swing my legs over the edge of my bed. "You win. I'm getting out of bed."

Nanna has tears in the corner of her eyes.

"Nanna don't cry. I've only got a headache."

Wiping her face, Nanna pats my hand. "Maybe Jack needs a day off school. He doesn't take days off often. And I'd like company today ..." Nanna's voice peters out. She looks at Mum, then at Grandad's photo on my wall. Mum puts her hands to her mouth and gives a small gulp. She looks at me, then Samantha.

"Both of you can take the day off. Be with Nanna. It's a special day. To remember Grandad." Mum puts her arm around Nanna. "Wish I could stay, but I have to work. I'm going to think about him all day."

I think about the date. Five years today. I feel his hand around mine like that last time.

Rob and Mum head off to work and Nanna gets busy.

She packs a bag of cookies, checks her handbag, and rattles her house keys before she drops them inside the bag to be lost forever between tissues and combs and lipstick and a photo album of us. She checks that her teeth are in, nods at me. "Time to visit Grandad."

Slinging my camera over my shoulder, I get a folding chair from the shed. I lean it against the wall, dig in my pocket for my phone and message Anna:

Jack: Won't be at school today. Seeing Grandad's grave with Nanna & Sammy. Can you tell Chris & everyone?

Anna: Oh Jack. Wish I could come.

Me too.

Samantha sits next to Nanna on the bus, holding the bag of cookies.

I stand, peering out of the window. "We're here." I point to the gravestones dotting the hill.

The bus jerks to a stop. Nanna nearly crashes to the floor, but I grab her arm, so she crashes into Samantha, who stops her from toppling over. "Are you OK?"

"Right as rain." Her eyes twinkle. "As long as you both are here." Samantha hugs Nanna, which is one of Nanna's favorite things in the world.

Puffing, Nanna waddles up the hill. Grandad's grave is right at the top, overlooking a bay. I unfold the chair next to it. "He always wanted a sea view. Now he's got one forever." She heaves herself into the chair then points to the cookies. "We can all have one. Oh, put out some for Grandad too. He'd like that."

"But the birds will eat them."

"Maybe he is a bird now." Nanna holds out her hand to the sky.

"He's an eagle, Nanna." I crumble some cookies and put them near the headstone. "He'd see everything from here."

"Grandad does see everything." Nanna smiles at me.

Nanna gets up from her chair and pulls out weeds from the side of his grave. Samantha and I help. A shadow ripples over the grass. I look up. A sea eagle is soaring above the hilltop, gliding right out to sea.

Nanna stands up. "Let's see where he's flying." She holds Samantha's hand. "Are you coming, Jack?"

"Just want to stay here for a while."

Nanna nods and wanders slowly away with Samantha. I watch the eagle, then take out my camera. He's like a king, gliding over hills, diving, swooping, climbing again. I zoom in until I feel like I'm flying with him. A pain shoots through my head and I let go of my camera. It drops, swinging from the straps. Holding my head, I lean on Grandad's grave. Whispering, I press my head against the stone. "Why are you here? Grandad, you promised you wouldn't leave me until I didn't need you anymore. I need you."

Chapter 16

Walk in My Shoes

"Missed you yesterday, Jack. Are you OK?" Mr. Angelou says.

"I'm OK, sir. Family stuff." He doesn't look sure. "I'm good, sir."

As soon as I get to my desk, Christopher whispers. "Your Grandad? Are you OK?"

I nod. I don't want to talk. I get out my pen. When I look up, Anna's turned around. She mouths. "Grandad?" I feel a lump rising in my throat.

"Ethics today. Open your work. *To Kill A Mockingbird*." Mr. Angelou waits until we're all paying attention then gives us a section to reread in groups. He wanders around making sure everyone's focusing.

After a while he sits down with the whole class and asks, "Why do you think that Atticus Finch, a white lawyer, defended a black man in a racist country town?"

George Hamel whispers, "He's color blind." Winger swallows a laugh, nudges Hawkie, who swallows a sneer, who nudges Paul, who pretends he didn't hear.

Mr. Angelou gives them a stare. "It's class time. Do any of you have an answer?"

George, Winger and Hawkie stop whispering. They shake their heads. "Jack. What do you think?"

Christopher swings his chair towards me. Why's Mr. Angelou asking me? I don't feel like talking or thinking about this now. Everyone's staring at me. I've got to say something. "Um, well. Atticus Finch, he's a quiet family guy, you know? A single dad in a small town where black people are treated unfairly. The white guys try to beat up this poor black man, who's just trying to look after his family. Atticus defends him because it doesn't matter what color you are. Everyone deserves a fair shot."

"That's right, Jack. Everyone deserves a fair shot." Anna smiles at me. That lump in my throat is rising again.

Mr. Angelou points to the board. *"You never really understand a person until you consider things from his point of view … Until you climb inside of his skin, walk around in it."*

"What does it mean, to 'climb inside of his skin, walk around in it'?" Mr. Angelou looks at Winger sitting next to him. "Winger?"

Winger has no idea. He shrugs. I squint at Hawkie with his bandaged nose, then at Christopher. Winger doesn't care.

"Come on. You're inside someone's skin. Standing in their shoes. What do you think?"

I fiddle with my pen. Shoes. I don't want to be in Christopher's shoes. He's scared. Rob's shoes? Mum's shoes? Nanna's? I've got to think. Do I want to even stand in *my* shoes? I have to find the answers.

The bell rings. Mr. Angelou sighs. "We'll continue this in our next ethics class."

Lunchtime. The new kid in class, Freddie, is standing at his desk holding his rugby ball. I can tell he doesn't know where to go or what to do. "Come on, Freddie. A pile of us are going to kick a ball around on the field. Touch rugby." He falls over his feet getting out from behind his desk. A yell comes across the room. "Freaky Freddie."

I turn around and yell back. "You're the freak." There're laughs and Freddie laughs too. "Come on, mate. Girls versus guys touch rugby." The girls are pretty good at kicking. I'm not a bad kicker either. I'm getting a bit sick of being in the reserves for rugby. Thinking of changing back to soccer. I'm good at that. Mum'll be happy. Rob won't. I don't want Rob to think I'm a loser.

I bite into my sandwich as we race ahead. Christopher stops. I stop. "What's wrong?"

"Forgot my lunch. Hey, but don't wait for me." He chucks the ball to me. "I'll be there soon."

"OK. Catch you in a minute." I wolf down the rest of the sandwich as I race with the guys to the field. I wave at the girls.

"Girls against boys," Maggie and Anna call out together.

"Haven't got a chance," I shout back.

The teams line up. Paul calls out. "There're more girls on their team. How unfair is that?"

"Chicken, eh?" Maggie hoots.

Paul and I crow together. "Watch out for the roosters."

"See who's crowing after the game," the girls shout back.

The coin's tossed. Anna calls heads. Girls win the toss. The ball's in play. There're kicks, runs, steals, passes. Anna kicks a huge one. Paul lunges and blocks. Cheers. Goal, goal, goal. Boys jump in the air, slapping hands.

Mrs. Banneker wanders over. She's on lunch duty. The ball's going fast down the line. Maggie's got it. "Go, girls," Mrs. Banneker shouts.

"Is that fair, Mrs. B?" I yell as I race to catch the girls.

"All's fair in love and war."

"But it's sports." I run backward raising my hands to Mrs. Banneker.

Eleven all. Mrs. Banneker points to her watch. "Bell's rung. Last play." The girls control the ball and run. Anna kicks a goal. Girls scream. Girls leap into each other's arms. I stand there stunned. Anna can do anything. What a kick. Then I grin: except maybe bat in cricket.

"Good play by everyone." Mrs. Banneker smiles. "Boys too."

I'm never going to see Mrs. Banneker in the same light. How's my work going to cope? As far as I can see, Ponto's a male. I'm shaking my head, when I suddenly remember. Where's Christopher? Oh, I see him coming our way. I race towards him. "What are you? A snail?" Christopher stares at his shoes. "You've missed the whole game." He looks up and I see it. A crack right across one lens of his glasses. "What happened?" Then I notice a red scrape right along his arm.

"It's nothing." He slides his arms behind his back.

I see Winger with George Hamel and their mates. "It's them, isn't it?"

Christopher shakes his head. "No."

"I'm going over. We can stand up together. They can't kill us."

"Don't, Jack. Don't." His voice cracks. "If you do, they'll do stuff."

"What can they do?" I head towards them.

Christopher grabs my shirt. "Don't. They've done it already. Painted ..." he stammers, "*chink* ... on the bakery wall again. My parents pretended that they weren't scared, but they were. It took them to bad places in Vietnam. To the war. We painted over it but ... they'll do it again. Please, just leave it. Please don't."

I stop. "Look, I've been there. We've got to do something."

"I know. Just not now."

We walk to the boys' bathroom. There're gravel bits and blood stuck in Christopher's elbow. He won't talk about what happened.

Ping. Ping. I look at my phone and frown. Facebook messages:

Legend: C betta now. 4 eyes.
Noddi: Saw arm?
Coola: Speling mate! Ha! Saw it off?
Likes: 22. Shares: 6.

Can't sleep. I'm on the computer searching. Where's my dad? I'm sick of dead ends. Go to bed. Can't sleep. Get up. Look through my telescope. There're lots of stars tonight. It's a half-moon. Go to bed. I close my eyes. All I can see is Christopher's broken black glasses. They look like monsters. I jump up. Anna's looking at me from my photo wall. I put my hand on her picture. I go back to bed, but this time it's the *pool*. George Hamel and Winger are there. The *pool*. I don't want to remember that day. What they did. Finally, I fall asleep.

Out of the pool. "Locker rooms," Mr. Angelou shouts. "You've got ten minutes." The showers, should I go in first? Second? Last? Mr. Angelou's shouting at us to move it. I head for the middle cubicle. The other boys jam into the other two cubicles and I can hear them throwing things and shouting. George Hamel's voice echoes against the walls. I can't help shuddering. Why do they hate me?

I'm alone in the middle cubicle. My head's throbbing. I get changed as quickly as I can. Panic. Don't cry, Jack. Don't. Almost dressed. A white blob catapults over the partition and slides down it. Another blob hits my back. I don't understand. Why? Why? Should I shout at them? Should I bang on the wall? But there's only me in here. What will I do? There's jeering. "Butt Head," "Butt Head," then a hailstorm of spit. I can't move. I can't breathe. It's so filthy. So disgusting. A big one lands on my shoe, splattering like egg white. I stare at my shoe. I grab my stuff and race out of the locker room.

***

Panting, I sit up, leaning on my hands. The *pool*. No one's ever going to bully me again. I can't stand by. Christopher's my mate. I've got to do something.

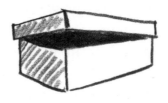

Chapter 17

The Shoe Box

What a rotten night. Glad Paul's doing the paper route this morning. Mum's gone already. She's dropping Samantha at her before-school gym class. Rob's left for work. It's just Nanna and me on the porch. Nanna sips her milky tea. I take out my camera. *Click, click, click.* A series of Nanna looking, smiling, thinking, sipping ... her wrinkly eyes, her hands around the teacup, her sore feet in sandals, the crinkles at the side of her mouth, the jam stain on her blouse, her locket with Grandad's picture.

"Are you wearing your purple undies, Nanna?"

She chuckles, flicking up her skirt. *Click. Click. Click.* Yes, they're purple.

As I head off, I look back at Nanna in the garden, watering the sunflowers and daisies. I'm so lucky she's here.

I arrive outside the Tran Bakery and wait for Christopher. He sticks his head out of the shop entrance. His glasses are still cracked. He jumps when he sees me. "It's just me. Thought I'd walk with you to the bus stop today."

He looks around for my tag-along sister. "Where's Samantha?"

"Before-school gym class. Mum dropped her off." He's still looking around. "There's no one else here."

He stammers. "I know that."

"Hey, Christopher. *I'm* here." He's quiet as we walk towards the bus stop. "My birthday invites are coming soon. They're pretty amazing, but I didn't make them. I'm not talented enough. The girl club did — Anna, Samantha, Nanna and Mum. They had fun doing it. Too much fun."

"I am glad." Christopher's speaking in a strange jerky way.

There are a couple of guys waiting for the bus. "Hey, let's stand over there." We plonk our bags in a quiet spot under a tree. "I'm showing Mr. Angelou the film of the game. The whole film. You've got to stand up for what's right." I wait.

"OK." I can hardly hear him.

"But I'm going to talk to George Hamel first. Winger and the other guys too, if I have to."

Christopher takes off his glasses and rubs them. His eyes are panicky. "Why are you doing that?"

"It's more than the scrum. It's your schoolbag! I've seen the messages too, Christopher. I know what they're doing." I don't say the words aloud — *four eyes, chink, slanty eyes.* "Let's talk to them. Get it over with." The bus appears at the end of the road, chugging towards us. Christopher doesn't answer. I pull his shirt. "So we're doing it?"

"Not today."

"When?"

"Tomorrow. Tomorrow."

"All right. We'll do it tomorrow."

Sports afternoon. Our bags are packed. We dump them at the locker rooms. I've been taken off the reserves bench at last. A real rugby game. It's not the 13As, but a game. Coach has discovered my "talent." Good, because my bum was getting sore just sitting on the bench. There's a yell. A whistle. Game's on. The ball's being passed along the line. Freddie's running fast. I'm like an eagle. The ball's coming my way. Pulse racing. Got to stop that ball going over the wrong line. I jump, sliding in the dirt, my arms outstretched. A save. A save.

Screams from my team. "Yeah, Jack. Yeah."

I give a thumbs-up. Maybe I'm good at this. I save a few more. Throw some good passes. Whistle. Yeah, our team wins. Slapping hands, we race off the field. "Great saves, Jack." I feel pretty good.

Slinging my bag over my shoulder, I jostle with everyone to the bus stop. I look around for Christopher at the bus line. He's not here. Paul runs up. "So you're not bad at rugby. Maybe you'll get on my team."

"I'm fine where I am." I look over at Hawkie. His nose isn't bandaged anymore, but he's still got two black eyes.

Paul pretend boxes me and we jump around, bumping into a few kids.

Mr. Angelou's voice booms across the bus line. "Hey, stop that."

I message Christopher:
    Jack: Where were you this after?
    Christopher: Went home sick. Flu.
    Jack: R U OK?
    Christopher: OK but have to take the rest of the week off.

It's late. I keep thinking about Christopher. As if he's sick. I check out my photo wall and move the photo of him in front of the Tran Bakery to the middle. Right next to Grandad in his army uniform.

I go to my desk. My computer screen stares at me like a brainless idiot. I press *Search*. No answers. More dead ends. My birth announcement comes up again and again. Yeah, I know, I know. I can't find my father. Where is he? Where? I hit my fist on the desk, turn off the screen and get up to go to the kitchen. Mum's baked another banana cake, since it's my favorite. I need a big piece. As I open my door, I see light coming from under Nanna's door. She might want a piece too. I call out, then knock, "Nanna. It's me."

"Come in, *me*."

Nanna's a joker too. She puts down her bridge book. She's already a champion. Smiling, she pats the chair next to her armchair. Puss investigates from the windowsill. Puss is always checking out the world. "Do you want some banana cake?"

"Hmm. Sounds delicious. With a cup of tea. But in a minute, Jack." She pats the chair next to her again. "It meant a lot that you came with me to see Grandad."

I sit down and lean towards Nanna. "Me too."

"You know how I said you can talk to him? And to me?" I nod. "It's sometimes really hard to talk, but I know there's something wrong. You were so quiet at the cemetery." I try to look down, but Nanna stares at me, right in the eyes. "I'm here. I don't know all the answers, or even any answers. But if we talk, maybe you'll find your own."

I can't tell Nanna about my nightmares. I can't tell her what I do every night at the computer. I shake my head. "I'm fine."

"Mum's excited about your birthday."

I groan. "Too excited."

Nanna gives me a knowing look. "Anna is too. She's such a dear girl."

I stammer. "I like her."

She puts out her hand to me. "I met your Grandad when I was at school. Though I was a bit older than you." Her eyes twinkle as she remembers. "You'll be thirteen very soon. That's such a special age. Trust me. What are you worried about?"

It's so hard to talk. I look at her. She watches me. "OK, Nanna. But you can't tell Mum. She's better now and she's happy with Rob. Her hair's grown back. You can never tell."

"I won't. I promise. You know I keep my word."

I take a breath. I stammer at first, then it comes like a river. Pouring, crashing out in a massive flood about Christopher, George Hamel, Winger — the pool, which is always in the corner of my mind. And how Mum could have died and I need to be there for her and my family and then I take a breath. But more comes out, about Grandad dying and leaving and Rob and no Dad.

Nanna listens until I don't talk anymore. We sit for a long time. Then she gets up and shuffles to her chest of drawers. She pulls out socks and purple underpants. I can't help smiling. Then she turns around, holding an old shoe box. She shuffles back to her armchair. "Your mum threw out these letters and documents eight years ago. There're photos, addresses. I've added things, when I've seen snippets in the newspapers, or overheard people talk. I've

written things down. Your mum doesn't know I have this box. But I kept it for you. For when you'd ask me." She hands me the shoe box.

My hands are shaking. "What's in here?"

"Take it back to your room. Open it. Talk to me when you're ready. I'll have the banana cake tomorrow, Jack."

Slowly I stand up, walk to the door, turn to Nanna. She nods and I leave holding the box. I get to my bedroom, slump onto my bed, lay the shoe box on my blanket. I take a deep breath and lift the lid. There're old papers. I shuffle through them. Cuttings from newspapers. Wedding notices with Dad's name crossed off. Mum must have been so scared. By herself. There's their wedding. I smile. Mum's wearing a hippie skirt that flounces with pale-yellow daises. She's wearing a daisy flower ring in her hair. Her blond hair is long with ringlets that go to her shoulders. Mum's beautiful. Then I stare at Dad. He's wearing gold square-framed glasses, a black suit with a purple velvet bow tie. I snigger. Who wears a purple velvet bow tie? I get up, walk around the room. I've been looking for him for so long.

There's shuffling down the corridor. I panic and throw my blanket over the box. *Woof, woof.* It's only Puppy racing to the flap door. I let out a breath and push the blanket away. More paper. Then I see it. I see it. Addresses. Boat Harbour. No, crossed out: not there. More addresses. No, not there. Not there. Not there. Then I see Nanna's scribbly writing. An address. A phone number. Not crossed out. He's there. Genoa Caves.

Chapter 18

Where's Four Eyes?

Genoa Caves. Can't stop thinking about it. Should I call? I have to, but when's the right time? What if Dad doesn't remember me? That's stupid. He'll remember me. I remember him. Got to talk to Nanna. Everyone's at breakfast and there's no time.

Nanna murmurs in my ear. "Do you want to have that banana cake tonight? Just us?"

"Yes. A lot of banana cake."

The school bus chugs along. Christopher isn't on it. I gaze out of the window. I jump when Anna taps me on my shoulder. "What do you think of yellow and blue streamers for birthday decorations? For under the shed awning?" I twist around. She beams like a sunflower. Samantha thumps the back of my seat.

"Fine." I'm totally uninterested. Anna's face drops and Samantha's thump deflates. "Oh, oh … sorry. Love streamers." Anna re-beams and Samantha re-thumps. They go back to chattering about my birthday. I go back to gazing out of the window until we reach school.

Classroom. I slide into my seat at my desk. Christopher's seat is empty. I watch the door. Maybe he'll come. He's not sick. *Ping. Ping.* Check my phone. Facebook messages:

Beast: Where's 4 eyes.

A photo of Christopher's broken glasses flash up.

Oki44: Whatcha call a FISH with no eyes?

      FSH!!!!!

Eagle: Christopha. Ha. fishface.

Likes: 9. Shares: 1.

I glare around the room. George Hamel's smirking, looking at Winger's knees. Winger's got to be Eagle. He's sending those fish jokes for sure.

The classroom door creaks open. Like lightning everyone turns off their phones: pings shut down all over the classroom. They're banned at school and doubly banned in class. We don't want our phones confiscated. It's a tough policy. Glad the school's grump handyman's so slack that he hasn't oiled the door's hinges. Mr. Angelou's bald head appears.

"Ethics today."

I can't think. Genoa Caves. Christopher. Dad. I pretend to write and keep my head down. Got to talk to George Hamel first. Then see what happens. My head's pounding.

Lunchtime bell. I stalk George Hamel all lunch. He doesn't see me. Ducking behind a tree, I watch him stuff down a sandwich with his mates. Then he's doing push-ups with Winger, Paul, his team at rugby practice. George has a lot of muscles. I check out his knuckles. Yeah, he's got muscles there too. All of a sudden, he jumps up and runs across the sports field. Where's he going? I follow him, dodging kids, hiding behind garbage cans. He's at the boys' bathroom. *Clang. Clang.* He belts the metal door as he bounds inside. Hanging near the benches outside, I wait and try not to look suspicious. My hands are sweating as I check, look around, check. *Clang. Clang.* I nearly jump out of my skin. George Hamel belts the metal door again and charges out of the bathroom. With the speed of light, I step in front of him. He lurches to a halt. "What the …?"

"Sorry, mate. Need to talk to you, George."

He puts his hands on his hips and we face each other. When did I get as tall as George Hamel?

Nausea grips my guts. I gulp. I remember George Hamel and his gang chasing me, sneering at me, "butt head," "butt head," and much worse. But that's over. The pool's over. That's not me anymore. I'm not taking it. I've got to do this for Christopher. For me. "It's the film clip of the rugby game. When you beat the Blues. Mr. Angelou wants to see it." My heart's pounding. I look George Hamel straight in the eyes. "To be fair, I want to show you first. There's stuff in it you'd want to see." I stand straight with my feet apart, cemented to the ground.

George Hamel squints towards the sports field. "I've got to get back to practice."

"So do ya want to see it or not?"

He squints at me now. "OK. After."

"Meet you at the side door."

George belts off. Casually, I wander towards the side door. A few kids yell out "Hi." I don't stop as I yell "Hi" back. I wait there. Wait. Wait. It's ages. Is he coming? Then I see him. He charges straight for me.

"This way." I open the side door and we creep into the corridor. It's out-of-bounds at lunchtime. We race towards our classroom. I look through the window to make sure Mr. Angelou or Mrs. Banneker aren't there. Empty. "Come on." We sneak inside. I take out my laptop from my bag and slide it onto my desk. George watches as I set it up. I press play. The school song and cheers blast into the classroom. We both jump. Quickly I push minus on the volume. The clip plays. George smirks as Becky screams "George, George, George," and Jasmin jumps. The film cuts to the game. Winger's running with the ball. George's leaping. Paul's passing. It's fast, fast, fast, broken up with shots of Mr. Angelou running with the game, the Coach yelling, "George: now. Now! Kill 'em. Kill 'em," and the cheering crowd.

The scrum takes up the whole shot. It moves like one massive beast. The ball's thrown in and the camera's inside the belly … then there's Hawkie and the blood.

We're dead silent, watching. When it ends, I look at George. He doesn't go ballistic. He doesn't say a word as I pack everything away. "We've got to get out of here," I whisper. I peer through the classroom window into the corridor to make sure no one's around. I creak open the door. I wish it didn't creak now. Then we run as fast as we can to the exit and we're outside and safe.

We look at each other. George grunts. "Let's talk, Jack."

"Library?"

"Yeah, sure."

Mrs. Lopez raises her eyebrow when she sees George Hamel and me together. "Are you OK, Jack?"

I nod at her. "Sure?" She gives George a suspicious look.

"I'm OK."

"Well, you know I'm here if you need me."

I smile at her. How'd anyone survive without the library? I look around at the books. There's my old spot in the science corner. "Over there." George follows me.

"You know the library pretty well, Jack."

"You should come in sometime." I scan the sports section as we walk past, and grab a book. *The Greats of Rugby*. "You'd like this one."

He takes it and flicks some pages as we walk. "Hmmm. Could do."

We drop into two beanbags. George Hamel leans back into his bag, puts the book on the floor and watches me. He's not giving me a free kick. He doesn't have to. It's my game. I've got to play this right. How do I even start? I close my eyes for a second, grit my teeth, then spit it out. "Winger's mean."

George Hamel laughs. "Yeah, he is sometimes."

"He's going for Christopher. Names. Fishface. Chink. Sending them out everywhere. Jokes that aren't funny."

"Yeah."

"There're photos. Messages. Facebook. Christopher's glasses. He can't see without them. The Tran Bakery had *chink* painted across it." I wait, look at George. I've got to do it. I've got to say. "You're in on it."

He punches his fist into his hand. I hide this gut-wrenching panic. I glance around. There's Mrs. Lopez.

"Nah. Just laughing along."

"That's how come they do it, George."

He grinds his fist into his eye socket. "Yeah, yeah. I know, OK. Look. I didn't know about the painting on the Trans' shop. I wouldn't do anything to Christopher myself. I don't do that stuff anymore." He rubs his hand across his forehead. "Ya know, I'm sorry. Sorry I did that garbage to you in the pool. Bullied you. I don't feel great about it. I don't want to do it anymore. To anyone." It's the first time he's really said sorry and meant it.

My panic subsides. I have to tell him. "You know I'll be showing Mr. Angelou the film clip."

George Hamel looks me in the eye. "Show it then. Winger needs a kick up the butt."

"He'll be in trouble."

"Yeah, he will."

"You could be too."

"I can take it. I'm the captain. Hawkie's our man. Should've told. Rugby's a good game. Got to keep it clean."

My head's spinning. George really is different.

"And what about Christopher?"

George Hamel shrugs. "OK, I'll get Winger to lay off Christopher. Everyone'll follow me. I know that."

"He can lay off everyone, right?"

George grunts. "Yeah, I'm gunna do it."

Mr. Angelou's sitting at his desk. "Sir." He peers up. "I've got the film clip of the game. Christopher and I put it together but ..." I stop. Nervously, I dig my hand in my pocket. I pull out the flash drive.

"Looking forward to seeing this."

I shuffle my feet uncomfortably.

Mr. Angelou puts the flash drive into his computer. He watches the game. Smiles. Then his face changes as Winger belts into the scrum. As Coach shouts in Hawkie's dripping face. Mr. Angelou puts his elbows on the desk and presses his chin against his knuckles. The clip ends. He sits there for a while, pushes his chair out, stands up, walks around his desk. He looks me in the eye. "I know this was hard to do. Thank you, Jack. Leave it to me."

Everyone's packing up. Principal Brown makes an announcement over the intercom. "Winger Ratko, Hawkie and George Hamel come to my office. Immediately." The principal's voice is angry.

Winger jumps. He grabs Hawkie's sleeve. "What've

you said? About the game?"

"I didn't say nothin'. My nose …" Hawkie's voice breaks.

"Shut up. Listen. Let's get our story straight." Winger glances at George Hamel, who's cool as a cucumber.

Winger is edgy and shoves Hawkie in the back as he heads out of the door. George Hamel looks back at me.

Chapter 19

Even If You Don't Win, How Can You Lose?

The classroom is strange this morning. Too many empty seats. Anna looks at me questioningly. I shrug, but I know it's about the scrum. George Hamel, Winger, Hawkie, Paul and anyone else on the team are missing.

Mrs. Banneker doesn't mention the missing boys. She just starts the math lesson. We're working on problems when George Hamel and his missing team arrive. They're very quiet. Mr. Angelou follows them in. "See you boys after school." He turns to Mrs. Banneker. "Would you mind if I give the class some homework?"

"Go ahead, Mr. Angelou."

He writes on the board:

In the end, it's extra effort that separates a winner from second place. But winning takes a lot more than that, too. It starts with complete command of the fundamentals. Then it takes desire, determination, discipline, and self-sacrifice. And finally, it takes a great deal of love, fairness and respect for your fellow man. Put all these together, and even if you don't win, how can you lose?

"That's from Jesse Owens, the grandson of a slave, a US Olympian. He won four gold medals in 1936. Copy it down. I want half a page on why fair play in sports is important. Use examples from the sports you play. Due tomorrow for our ethics class."

Mr. Angelou gives Winger a direct look. "I'd expected a lot more from you and the whole team. We'll be talking about this with Coach after school."

Mr. Angelou nods at me. I nod back.

It's a weird day. Too much to think about. After school, I'm going to drop in on Christopher. At lunchtime, I race to the library. Mrs. Lopez is happy to see me. "If you need anything, I'm here." Samantha's dog project is still on display with her blue first-prize ribbon. I walk around it and it's actually really good. Apart from the pre-plastic-surgery elephant nose, Samantha got it right. I find one of the supersize atlases and follow the route from home to Genoa Caves.

Luckily afternoon class is art. I like art, but today I like it even more because we're outside sketching. I disappear behind a huge fig tree with my pencils and paper. I sketch black glasses. A lot of them. Then a man. You can only see his back, the back of his head, his hands. I let my pencil slide off the page, close my eyes and rest against the tree. The end of day bell goes.

Mr. Tran smiles when he sees me enter the bakery after school. "Come to visit Christopher?" he waves me through. "Christopher is upstairs in his room. He's sick."

Mrs. Tran notices me from the storeroom and calls out. "Hello, Jack."

I shuffle through the shop and climb the stairs to Christopher's room. I knock as I enter. Christopher turns around from his desk. He pretends to cough. He's got a new, uncracked lens in his glasses.

"You can see again. I've got something for you." Rummaging through my bag, I pull out my birthday invitation. "Everyone's got theirs already. Left it in their desks, but you haven't been at school." He opens it and puts it down.

I sit on his bed. "Are you feeling better?" I know he's not sick.

"Yeah." Christopher gives another cough.

"I showed George Hamel the clip of the game. He was OK about it." I grin. "He said Winger's a bum. And Hawkie shouldn't have been treated like that by Winger and the Reds."

"Really?"

"Really. He sort of admitted that he was a jerk last year. He knew I was going to show Mr. Angelou. George said that's OK. I couldn't believe it. I guess people can change if they want."

"What about Winger?"

"George said he'd tell him to lay off you. George wasn't involved in the graffiti."

"Do you believe him?"

"Yeah, I do, and they'll be on detention for a long time."

Christopher takes off his glasses and rubs the new lens. "School's really important to my parents. To me too. I don't know how long I could've stayed away."

"So you weren't sick?" I nudge him.

"Funny." He swallows hard. "Thanks, Jack."

"Yeah, I've learned you can't do everything alone. So you'll be at school tomorrow?"

"I'll be there."

It's good to get home. Samantha's cutting sunflowers for the house. She waves them at me. Puppy's chasing his tail. Ollie's digging holes in the flower beds. Nanna's cutting back the roses.

I walk up behind Nanna. "Nanna, can I talk to you?"

She jumps back and screams. "You gave me a fright." She puts down the gardening scissors. "Let's go to the porch." When we make it up the stairs she sits in a garden chair. I put down my bag and sit next to her. "What do you want to talk about?" Her eyes crinkle shut, then open. She knows what.

"It's the shoe box. He lives in Genoa Caves. Just three hours away. There's a phone number."

"What do you want to do, Jack?"

"I don't know."

"I think you do, Jack." She puts her hand over mine. The softness sends a wave of Nanna through me.

"Can't hurt Mum. She's always been here for Sammy and me. Dad just left. Never heard from him again. What if it's the wrong thing to do?"

"We all have to make choices."

I rub my head. "I want to call him. To ask him things."

"Then you'll have your answers."

Rob's yellow van toots, blasting "Surfer Joe" down the driveway. Mum sticks her head out of the car window. She's waving glow sticks. "Birthday express, coming through." She's raided the discount shop. Streamers, streamers and more streamers. Balloons, balloons and more balloons. I go to help carry some of the bags. "Mum, is there anything left at Susie's Super Discount Store?"

"Your birthday's important, Jack. Come on, everyone, let's get it all sorted and packed away."

Rob's stacking boxes of drinks in the shed. Nanna's found the Hawaiian leis. There must be a hundred of them. Samantha's discovered the sparklers. "Mum, I love them. Can we try some now?"

Mum does a little twirl. "Why not? I love them too."

Samantha and Mum dance around making sparkling flowers in the air. Got to get my camera.

Night. I have to make the call. I start pacing across my bedroom. I sit down, get up, pace some more, stop. Got to call. I get on to my computer and search for the hundredth time, Genoa Caves. It flashes up. Three hours' drive, into the mountains. It's on the train line. I open Nanna's box again, rummage through the papers and photos. There it is. The phone number in her shaky writing. I take it out and flatten the page with the palm of my hand. I've got to phone, but my hand is shaking. Stop shaking, Jack. What am I? A coward? I stare at the photo of

144

Grandad. Do it, Jack. Do it. I feel like I'm choking. I press the numbers. *Ring, ring, ring.*

There's a pickup. A man's voice. "Hello." My throat's dry. I cough. The man's voice asks, "Is someone there?"

I cough again. "Yeah. Dad. It's me. Jack."

There's a gasp from the other end, then a jerky question. "How have ya been, Jack?"

"I don't know. Good, I suppose."

"I thought one day you'd call, Jack."

"I thought one day you'd call, Dad."

Chapter 20

Plans Afoot

Nanna's door is open. She's waiting for news. I pad into her room. Tears dot the corners of my eyes. I rub my face. "Nanna, I'm seeing him. Dad." That word feels unreal. Dad. Have I really got a dad? "You promised to help me, Nanna. We've got to do this." My breath becomes short. "You can't tell Mum. Or anyone. I've never really lied to her before, but we need to do this."

"Mum will understand if we talk to her. We should." Nanna hesitates. "I've never lied to her before either."

Guilt alert. Nanna's weakening. She wants to tell. I use the Caring Strategy. "We're protecting her. She'd feel bad. Really bad."

Nanna's Care Factor is triggered. Her eyes shimmer. "Yes, we've got to protect her."

We make the deal. Nanna and I are agents on a mission. She's been briefed. Saturday is our target date. Dad's expecting me. He asked about Samantha. She's off-limits. Destination locked-in. Genoa Caves.

"Ready to go to dinner?" I give Nanna the sign. Thumbs-up. She returns it. Thumbs-up. Mum's singing as she dishes out pasta. Rob ladles out parmesan cheese. He sits down at the table next to Samantha. Dinner is normal. Well, for our family, which means Mum's forcing us to have celery or carrot juice. We've all picked carrot. Mum's gulping down celery. Poor Mum. She's trying to show us how good it is. We're not fooled. Rob's shaking, barely controlling his laughs.

Nanna deploys her secret weapon. Freshly baked chocolate chip cookies from the Tran Bakery. She brings them out right on time. Hands them around. Everyone's munching, even Ollie and Puppy. Samantha smuggles some illegal bits under the table. This is called softening up the opposition. Nanna waves her cookie in the air. "Everyone, I've an announcement." Heads turn to her. "Jack and I want to spend some special grandson–Nanna time together."

Mum melts. "Lovely."

Nanna and I lock eyes. Our plan. "This Saturday."

Mum's voice is gushy. "Saturday? Lovely."

"In the mountains. Genoa Caves."

"The mountains? Genoa Caves? That's too far. For just one day? I don't think it's a good idea."

I eyeball Nanna. She tries the Guilt Strategy. "Are you saying I'm not capable of going on a train ride there?"

Mum is flustered. "No, no. You'll enjoy the trip."

Then the worst happens. I hadn't thought about it. It's Samantha. "What about me? Aren't I a grandchild? Don't I matter?" Her bottom lip's trembling.

Nanna's face crinkles into worry lines. "You matter a lot, Samantha."

Mum gives Nanna a look. "It'd be lovely if Samantha could go with you."

Oh no. This is going all wrong. Samantha's upset. I've got to fix it. "Sammy. I wasn't thinking. I really want you to come to the mountains. Nanna does too." Samantha glances at Nanna who's nodding. "We're the three amigos. Nanna, you and me."

She looks up. "Really?"

"Yeah. It wouldn't be much fun without you. Nanna thinks that too."

Rob puts his hand on Samantha's shoulder. "You'll like the mountains."

"We're the three amigos, Sammy." How am I going to do this? I look at Sammy laughing. She's got to come. I'll figure it out.

Christopher is nervous when he goes into our classroom.

Anna calls out, "Glad you're better."

He smiles.

"Nice glasses," Winger sneers. We move on towards our desks. George gives me a quick nod and then bashes Winger's arm. Winger retreats into his seat and pretends it's all a joke. George Hamel's keeping his promise. He's right. Winger's a bum. I don't trust Winger and he's not going to win, not now that George is on it. And Mr. Angelou is on it.

It's hard to concentrate at school. All I can think about is tomorrow. The trip to Genoa Caves. I don't want to be at school today.

I can hear only when Anna's talking to me. "So why are you really going to Genoa Caves?"

I flinch. How does she know there's another reason? I'd lie to her, but she'd never forgive a lie. I notice Paul. Quick plan. "Anna, have to tell Paul something. Sorry, got to go." I race off. "Paul. Paul." I look back: Anna's still watching me.

Everything's so confused in my head. I don't even know if I want to see Dad. He hasn't called me in five years. There's Rob too. The day is a blur. Final school bell. I thought it'd never ring. We're off the bus and walking home. Christopher stops outside the bakery. We knuckle touch. "Thanks, Jack."

Anna and I walk towards the Napolis' Super Delicioso Fruitology Market. "You'd tell me if something was happening, wouldn't you?" She hesitates. "You're my best friend."

"Better than Maggie?" I joke.

"Better than Maggie." She stops. All I can see are her dark beautiful eyes.

I stammer. "There is something. I promise I will tell you. But not yet. I can't lie to you. You're my best friend too. Trust me."

She thinks for a while, then says seriously, "All right, Jack." She holds out her hand. I take it and we walk home.

Saturday. Rob's running around. He's made romantic plans with Mum. Mum's going to get her fingernails and toenails painted and her hair styled this morning. Rob doesn't need anything more done to his hair. Ha. He's booked a lunch boat cruise. Then a movie in the luxury class where they get champagne. Mum's choice of movie. No surfing or action heroes or bomb blasts. Rob even said Mum could pick a love story.

I'm trying not to laugh. "Hey, Mum. I thought we're the most important people in the world to you? It looks like you're glad to get rid of us."

Mum's face scrunches into worry lines. "No, it's just ..."

My self-control bursts. I splutter, "It's OK, Mum. We know you love us."

Rob's standing at the van. "Ready?" he sings out. Nanna pads outside, carrying her special large bag. There'll be cookies, apples, drinks in it, for sure. *Be prepared* is her motto. She's a Girl Scout at heart. Samantha follows. I check my camera. Nanna's in the front seat. Samantha and me in the back. We wave madly at Mum as the van rattles away.

We board the train, get seats facing each other. Nanna unpacks supplies. I was right. Cookies. Samantha chatters to Nanna. Glad she's here. I don't want to talk. I take photos as the town disappears and we rattle through fields, other towns, more fields, into mountain trees, climbing into the mountains. Samantha stops talking and plays with her game. Nanna's asleep. I click photos of her with her soft cheeks and graying hair.

Towering fir trees rise on either side of the tracks as the train clacks upward. It starts to wind around the mountains. Valleys drop and I get glimpses of a river. It's photo heaven with the sunlight streaking through the clouds.

The train starts to slow. Samantha puts away her game. Nanna must have a sixth sense, as she suddenly wakes up. "Are we here?" I nod. "Lovely trip." As if Nanna would even know.

I peer through the window. "We're here. Genoa Caves."

Chapter 21

We're a Team

Nanna sways as we walk through a rocky cavern. Dripping crystal stalactites hang like ice from its roof. Samantha yelps when a drip splashes onto her hand. A stream runs through the cave. We lean over the railing to see where the river goes. It just disappears into a dark hole. What's under us? Where's it going? I stare down.

"The guided tour starts in a minute. The Grand Cave. You'd better get in line." I glance at the time. "And I've got to go."

"Aren't you coming, Jack? The Grand Cave. You have to come —"

I cut her off and lie. "I'm not missing out, Sammy. I'm doing the rock climbing one."

"Oh, that'll be good too." Samantha smiles.

Nanna presses her hand against my arm. "You be careful."

"I will. See you in a couple of hours and don't fall into a crack, Nanna. Sammy."

Nanna and Samantha line up for the Grand Cave tour. I look at the time, then check my camera and pull my backpack onto my shoulders. I walk, then start jogging back through the cave to the road. The cliffs are huge. I half expect to see the ocean, but these cliffs plunge into wilderness and rocky outcrops. I see the snaky river deep in the valley. A shadow glides above. I look up and see a gray–brown eagle soaring. Grandad?

The wooden cottages huddle together. My heart's jumping. I press my hands against my legs. Come on, Jack. You can do this. A man hangs over the railing of the last

cottage. It's got to be him. I know it's him. I'm going to be sick. My legs feel stuck, feet glued to the ground.

The wind whistles and I know Grandad's next to me. "We're a team, Jack. We can depend on each other. Let's do this together."

"OK, Grandad."

The man jerks up his head as I walk towards him. It's him. I remember. Two trail bikes are in the front. I pass them and climb up the wooden steps. I'm not scared. I'm not scared, Grandad. No one can make me scared.

"Hi, Jack."

"H-hi," I stammer. "Dad?"

"Glad you could come, Jack." He stands up from the railing.

My heart pounds. He's got brown hair like me. Brown eyes. A jacket like the one he always wore. It's him. Really him. I walk up the steps.

"Good weather," he says.

"Yeah. Good weather."

There's a table set up with a jug of lime cordial, a bowl of chips and a bowl of nuts. "Let's sit down. Here's a drink." He pours a glass for me, then himself.

"So how's things, Jack?"

"OK. How's things with you?"

"OK."

This is so uncomfortable. I slide looks at him. I can just about remember him.

"Glad you're here, Jack."

I swallow. "What do you do?"

"I'm a builder. Do you like building things?"

"Yeah. I like taking photos." I pull out my camera. "Can I take a photo?" He nods and I *click, click, click*.

He starts talking. I listen. He likes the wilderness, camping at night under the stars, the caves. He makes things like I do, but he doesn't surf. "What about you, Jack?"

I shrug but the question's burning inside me. I have to ask. "It took me a very long time to find you. I didn't know where you were, but you always knew where I was." I look him in the eye. "Why didn't you come back?"

He rubs his hands, stares at his dusty boots, then me. "Because I had a new life. There was someone else. It was easier to pretend you weren't there." He presses his fingers against each other. "And the longer I didn't see you … It just got easier to forget."

That really hurts. "It was hard for Mum. And us."

He nods. "It's not good enough. I know that. But you're braver than me. And you're here now, Jack. And there's Sammy. How is she?"

My head's spinning. I blurt out, "She loves dogs."

He looks over at the trail bikes. I look over too.

One's just right for a kid. "Matt loves dogs too." He bites his lip. "I've got … a boy. A son. Matt. He's eight."

A boy. He has a son. But I'm your son. You left me and told me to be good.

"I'd like to get to know you. And Sammy."

"Maybe. Got to go." I don't call him Dad.

"See you again, Jack."

"Sure."

Dazed, I walk back to the Grand Cave. Nanna and Samantha are waiting. Samantha talks nonstop about the Grand Cave. I'm glad she's talking, because I can't. Nanna shuffles close to me.

The train rattles through the mountains. It's dark by the time we reach the plains on the way home. I take out my camera and look at my photos. Dad's face, again and again.

The train pulls into Boat Harbour. Mum and Rob are waiting for us on the platform. Nanna nearly stumbles as she gets off, but Rob's there and steadies her. Samantha's bursting with news. She shows Mum the Genoa Caves guidebook Nanna bought for her.

Mum's glowing, with a daisy chain woven into her hair. "Woooh. The hairdresser did a great job." Mum smiles and I hug her for a very long time.

Chapter 22

Endless Summer

Rob and I set up the tent in the garden, as well as the screen and sound system inside it. We're slick and fast. It's all our practice working together. Mum keeps coming out with drinks. She's the support crew.

Next job is the barbecue. Rob's on it and it's a miracle. It's working. Puppy has been banished to the shed since he weed on Rob's shoe. He gets too excited. Ollie's in there too, keeping him company.

Mum and Nanna are in a cooking frenzy. There're going to be a lot of banana cakes.

Rob collects Leo from the train station. He arrives just in time to join "Operation Balloon." He chucks his backpack into my room, puts on his Hawaiian shirt, waves to everyone and gets on board. Anna and Samantha have blown up so many balloons that the backyard looks like an overfed-confetti explosion. Anna and Samantha are now twisting ribbons on the last of the balloons. Leo's slotted in. His job is to hand the ready-to-go balloons to me. My job is to not fall off the ladder while I hang them. I'm not doing a bad job knotting the balloons under the shed awning.

Rob calls out to all of us. "Great work."

Mr. Tran has just dropped off Christopher. He's looking good in his "hang five" T-shirt. I clamber down the ladder and help Mrs. Tran with the rolls she's brought. Enough for the whole street.

Ping. Ping. I dig my phone out of my pocket. Message from George Hamel. What's he want?

George Hamel: it's yur birthday mate. Hav a good one. C ya at the surf.

I hold my phone for a while.

Jack: Thanx. C ya there.

I look up. Puppy and Ollie have been let out of the shed and found a balloon. It's going to burst. I'm right. It does. They run for cover. Surfing songs rock through the backyard. *The Endless Summer* is playing. Rob's put up the twinkling lights. Mum hula dances onto the porch in a pink sarong and top. No snapdragons, luckily. Rob whistles. She does a quick jumping jack.

"Better get ready myself." I clear three steps in one go and race to my bedroom. Mum bought me an orange surfer T-shirt. It's bright. You need sunglasses just to wear it. I drag it over my head. It'll make Mum happy. My board shorts look good. "Hey, Hector, maybe you should be giving me a crumb today, since it's my birthday." Ponto's starting to be a real vegetable. Never know, I could be a real scientist one day. What do ya think, Einstein? I glance at his photo. Reckon he's nodding his head. Anna's beautiful eyes stare at me from my photo wall. Hope she likes the shirt.

I look at the bottom of the wall. I unpin the photo of my father and us. Staring at it, I flop onto my bed. I hold the one card without a return address and with the postmark "Genoa Caves." I was waiting to open it today. I look around my room, at Grandad's medals, my camera, telescope, my soccer ball, my experiments on the windowsill. I tear the envelope. It's an ordinary card. There's a photo of a rugby ball, sports car and a teenage guy. I look inside.

To Jack — Happy 13th birthday. Dad.

An envelope falls out. Tearing the corners, I lift the flap. There's a photo of him and Matt, and some money.

"Dad." I say it aloud, repeating it. "Dad. Dad. Dad." He doesn't feel like a dad. I'm going to have to tell

Mum I've seen him. But not now. It's *my* party. I run my fingers through my hair, straighten my shirt, look in the mirror. I dash down the hallway to my family. Rob and Mum turn around.

"Wow." Rob jumps back. "That's bright."

"Mum bought it for me."

Rob glances at Mum. "It's fantastic." We look at each other and splutter.

"You can laugh, but I love the T-shirt." Her eyes go teary. "I can't believe you're thirteen. Thank you for wearing it, darling."

"Mum, don't call me darl—" I stop. Then smile. "It's going to be a great party."

Anna floats towards me in a misty-blue sarong, and white tank top, her dark curls threaded with white frangipanis. "Can I show you something?" I nod, following her across the grass, past the flowerbeds and garden chairs. Under the twinkling lights behind the tent she hands me a small blue box. "For your birthday, Jack."

I lift the lid. The round silver medal shines on the navy velvet bed. *Peace, Paix, Pax* is written in tiny letters inside the circle of doves of a 1971 United Nations Peace Medal. I look into her dark eyes. I take her soft hands and hold them in mine. She looks up at me. I bend my head towards her and we kiss in the moonlight.

Chapter 23

Thirteen

"People coming," Samantha shouts from the back porch. Nanna smiles comfortably in her chair, patting Puss. She's got the best seat in the house.

Oh, it's Paul. He swings through the front gate and saunters towards me. I race up with Leo tagging along. "Hey, Paul. Oh, here's Leo. He's come down from the north for the party. He's not a bad surfer."

"Can't have too many surfers."

I see Rob from the corner of my eye. "Right. And he's my stepbrother."

Maggie and a heap of girls suddenly arrive from nowhere. Anna runs over to them. "You look fantastic, Anna. Your sarong!" Maggie squeals.

"You look great too. Those bangles are amazing. I love the green spangles. The pink ones are gorgeous. Oh, the gold ones ..." Anna's working up Maggie's arm.

Girl talk. I'm out of here. I skim past the pile of presents on the table set up by Mum. "Hey, Rob, like your hat." Yep, he's wearing his *The World's Greatest Cook* hat. And the apron too. "Burning the sausages?"

"No way." He's seriously concentrating on turning them.

There's a major watermelon basket in the middle of the table decorated with frangipanis and hibiscus. Mum's majorly proud of it. She has a second one in the kitchen. I grab a chunk of watermelon.

I check out Christopher, who's taken on the role of DJ. There're girls hanging around him. "Turning from nerd to girl magnet, hey. What happened?"

He shrugs, smiling. "Don't know, but I'm keeping this job." He puts on "Limbo Rock" and the party's on.

The limbo stick gets lower and lower as everyone bends back far enough to get under it. Lots of collapses. Maggie crashes onto the grass, giggling. Oh, Leo's grabbed her hand to pull her up. Oh no, Mum's dragging Rob into the line. "Go on, Rob." Mum flounces around. "Hmmm. OK, for you, babe." Rob stretches, then bends backward. Clapping erupts and he throws his arms in the air. "The old surfer's got a bit of life in him yet." He laughs.

"Do it again, Dad, but lower." Leo shoves him. There's jumping and yelling.

"Yeah, Dad." I flinch. "I mean Rob." Rob turns to me. "Yeah," I pause. "Dad." It feels hard to say that, but all right. It's all right.

"OK, I'll show you clowns how it's really done." There're cheers and jeers. He bends back low and shuffles towards the limbo stick.

I take out my camera and crouch down. *Click.* The back of Rob's head bobbing low to the ground.

Click. Sammy, jumping up and down. "Come on, Dad. You can do it."

Click. Everyone pumping their arms in time to "Surfin' USA."

Click. Rob giving a winner yell and pumping his arms with them.

The sausages are a hit. Rob's king of the barbecue. The watermelon basket's a hit. Mum's in heaven. Then the drum roll. Christopher hits "Happy Birthday."

In a blaze of candles, Mum's face shines as she carries the birthday cake outside. Yep, it's a surfboard cake. Rob and Leo walk behind her carrying a brand-new surfboard. Rob gives me the thumbs-up. "Happy birthday, Jack."

The singing is loud. Paul leads the second verse of "Happy Birthday to You," finishing with:

*You look like a monkey
and you smell like one too.*

I blow out the candles with one massive breath. Cut the cake. My knife touches the plate and comes out covered in cake.

"That means you've got to kiss the girl nearest you," Mum sings. I give Mum a don't-do-this stare. Mum couldn't care less and takes a step further away from me.

"Oooohhhhh. Get movin', Jack," Paul yells. Anna's standing there looking beautiful and trying not to laugh.

"What are you waiting for? Next birthday?"

"Whoa."

"She won't bite."

"Ha-ha-ha-ha-ha-ha-ha."

"Shut up, everyone." I give Anna a quick kiss.

Cheering erupts and I glance over at the porch. Nanna's eyes are soft and twinkling. Beside her is Grandad.

I take Anna's hand and she presses mine. I look around. Yeah, being Jack's OK. I smile.

Author Susanne Gervay:

Sydney's my home with the harbor, beaches, Centennial Parklands and my two kids. My "I Am Jack" series is inspired by my family, friends, community and real stuff that happens. Nanna buys everyone underpants and socks, even though we wish she wouldn't. Jack's sister loves dogs and doing her hair. She's got a big heart. Rob is a maniac dishwasher. We visit Grandad's grave and share secrets with him. It's important to us. Jack is my son and he's very funny, or thinks he is. He's such a great kid.

But life gets complicated sometimes, with blending families, bullying, getting sick, schoolwork. Jack made it through bullying and stands up for himself and others now. However, books are a safe place to find friends and work out answers. Jack likes his books. I do too. That's why I support libraries, literacy and Room to Read.

I love that my "I Am Jack" books are published and translated all over the world and that *I Am Jack* has been adapted into a play by Monkey Baa Theatre. I hope Jack is your friend. He's mine.

Website: www.sgervay.com
Blog: www.sgervay.com/blog
Room to Read: www.roomtoread.org
Monkey Baa Theatre: www.monkeybaa.com.au

Interested in learning more about cricket or rugby?

The United States of America Cricket Association
http://www.usaca.org/

Cricket Australia
http://www.cricket.com.au/

USA Rugby
http://usarugby.org/

National Rugby League (Australia)
http://www.nrl.com/

Room to Read®

About Susanne Gervay and Room to Read

Susanne Gervay OAM is a committed writer ambassador for Room to Read, an innovative global nonprofit that seeks to transform the lives of millions of children in ten developing countries in Asia and Africa through its holistic literacy and girls' education programs.

Working in collaboration with local communities, partner organizations and governments, Room to Read focuses its efforts on developing reading skills in primary-school children because literacy is the foundation for all future learning. Since it was founded in 2000, Room to Read has impacted the lives of over 9 million children by establishing school libraries, publishing original children's books in more than 25 local languages, constructing child-friendly classrooms and supporting educators with training and resources to teach reading, writing and active listening.

As Susanne says, "With a dedication that I have rarely seen, with an organizational structure that has integrity and is collaborative with families and communities, Room to Read changes the future of kids trapped in poverty. Through education and books, Room to Read gives disenfranchised children a precious gift, so they can move out of poverty to be all they can be. It changes their lives and the world."

For more information, visit www.roomtoread.org.